BRIGHT-EYED AND
BUSHY-TAILED

FAIRY TALES OF A TRAILER PARK QUEEN
BOOK 11

KIMBRA SWAIN

Kimbra Swain
Bright-Eyed and Bushy-Tailed, Fairy Tales of a Trailer Park Queen, Book 11
©2019, Kimbra Swain / Crimson Sun Press, LLC
kimbraswain@gmail.com

ASIN: B07NNCB9TL
ISBN: 978-1796697056

Book Cover by: https://www.ts95studios.com

Formatting with the help of Serendipity Formats: https://serendipityformats.wixsite.com/formats

Editing by Carol Tietsworth: https://www.facebook.com/Editing-by-Carol-Tietsworth-328303247526664/

A NOTE FROM THE AUTHOR

Bright-Eyed and Bushy-Tailed was a phrase used by my grandmother on the days I'd spend the night at her house. My parents worked several jobs each, and I spent a lot of time with my grandparents. I remember my MawMaw saying it in the mornings, because I wasn't a morning person. I'm still not a morning person, but I can hear her saying it in my head.

This story within the Trailerverse, as it is now being called, is a lighthearted fun tale of a Yeti and a plague of squirrels. The idea to having attack squirrels steamed from two things. First, I have had one in my attic several times, and the scratching can be utterly annoying. I needed something silly and annoying to interrupt Grace and Levi's plans for battle, as well as, their personal endeavors.

Secondly, as any student or alum from the University of Alabama knows, there is a species of squirrel known as the Quad Squirrel. They are huge, and the area known as the Quad on the UA Campus is their home. If you try to sit on their benches, they will run you off. If you try to sit on their lawns, they will attack. They are not afraid of humans at all. The bushy-tailed, beady eyed varmints are well known for their territorial ways. Since, Fairy Tales of a Trailer Park Queen takes place in Alabama, I thought it only fitting that we have at least one episode of Quad Squirrels.

In the beginning of this book, Grace talks about a trip to Vegas. It is a fun short story that I wrote as a Christmas gift to my reader group, Magic and Mason Jars. Jingle in Your Jangle features Grace, Levi, and Tennyson as they dip into the Las Vegas underworld which is manned by a mob boss who is a frog. They are helped by a vampire pirate named Seamus. The vampirate, as he has been lovingly dubbed, will be a recurring character in a series that I will launch this fall focusing on Winnie.

While in Vegas, Grace finds out that her mother, as well as, some of the other fairies from the Winter Otherworld have escaped Brockton's wrath. However, they are unable to find out any other information.

Jingle in Your Jangle can be found in my reader group: Magic and Mason Jars on Facebook.

Kimbra Swain's Magic and Mason Jars

I hope you enjoy Bright-Eyed and Bushy-Tailed. There are four books left in the series, and not every moment will be happy moments. There will be laughs. There will be tears. This is a light-hearted in-between book.

Welcome to the 11th edition of Fairy Tales of a Trailer Park Queen. Pull up a chair, grab a glass of sweet tea (or orange soda), and get lost inside Shady Grove once again.

CHAPTER ONE

BRIGHT MORNING SUNSHINE POURED THROUGH THE GAUZY CURTAINS
as I rolled over alone in bed. Levi had been gone all night chasing
griffins. One of our newer citizens just happened to be a griffin
breeder. We allowed it as long as it didn't turn into one of those
puppy factories that you see on the sad commercials on television.
Madam Luella Specter moved here with four griffins. Three males
and one female. The female was a feisty thing and frequently kicked
the male griffins out of the pen. In turn, the mayor and the police
chief would spend half the night chasing the winged creatures.
They took Aydan with them this time thinking that he might offer
some help corralling the creatures. Apparently, he didn't since they
were both gone all night. We might have to invoke some sort of
griffin ordinance to force Madam Specter to keep her tots in line.

Above my head, an incessant scratching continued in the attic.
Levi had climbed up there yesterday to see what sort of critter had
found its way into the empty space above the house. He couldn't
find anything using his sight. It was annoying, to say the least.

I felt Levi arrive outside the house with Aydan. Callum was with
them as well. I figured he had gone with them, but I wasn't sure. He
had been spending time with Dominick and the wolves, too. It was

1

good for him to keep those ties. He may not have been the same species as the lycans in Troy's pack, but they were as close to family as he would find, besides Aydan.

Hearing their voices, I tried to force myself to crawl out of bed. Since we had returned from Las Vegas at Christmas, there had been one small crisis after another. Which meant, Levi and I hadn't had the chance to spend any time alone. Winnie went through three weeks of what Wendy called Phoenix sickness. She had chills and a cough. I figured it was a cold, but Wendy explained that because I had made her a fairy, that she had some winter in her that battled with the fire from her father. Tabitha had disagreed on the diagnosis saying she felt like it was remnants of Winnie's human parts picking up a common cold. I didn't know what to think other than I hated seeing my child suffer. She spent most of her nights in bed with me. Thankfully, she was finally feeling better.

Bramble's shrill voice piercing through the air swept away any sleepiness that still lingered, while Rufus barked incessantly.

"Avast, ye land lubber! I shall wound thee with my cutlass!" he shouted.

Winnie started giggling, then Briar joined the shouting, "Get your fairy ass back down here! That creature will eat you whole!"

"No, my love, I shall tar and feather this beast in your honor," Bramble insisted.

"What the ever-loving hell is going on?" I shouted at the door.

"What are y'all doing?" Levi asked outside my door.

Grabbing the robe beside my bed, I wrapped it around myself and opened the door to see Winnie standing at the bottom of the pull-down ladder that stretched up into the attic. Briar and Thistle held on to each other as they hovered just above her head. Levi and Aydan came up the steps from the first floor staring up into the ceiling.

"The beast has awakened me every night with its constant scratching! I must get my beauty sleep. And my poor Bramble has gone into the war. He's a lover not a fighter. He will die, then I will have to find a new prick," Briar exclaimed. She sounded like Scarlett O'Hara right after Ashley Wilkes rejected her.

"Briar," I scolded her.

"It's okay, Momma. I know what a prick is," Winnie said, as Rufus continued to bark.

"Knowing it and saying it are two different things!" I protested. "Rufus! Hush! I'm gonna feed you to the wolves if you don't quit that harfing!"

"Okay," Winnie said, staring up into the attic waiting for some sign that Bramble had survived his battle.

"Morning," Levi said, leaning over to kiss my cheek.

"All-nighter?" I asked.

"I'd say yes, but we aren't talking about the same thing," he grinned.

"Maybe we are," I replied. He grunted and groaned at the same time. It was a groant.

"King Levi, if you would please aid my dear mate as he's gotten himself in a pickle," Briar said.

"I'm pretty sure it's not a pickle," Winnie said.

"No, but he's been in a pickle before," I replied. Levi grinned, and Briar winked at us.

"Arrgh!" Bramble exclaimed from the darkness of the attic. "Give me all your gold you rotten sack of potatoes!"

"Why does he sound like a pirate?" I asked.

"Role-play," Briar explained. "He takes his art very seriously."

"Nevermind. I don't want to know," I said, holding up my hands before she could continue to explain. I was already sorry I'd asked.

"Does he rape and pillage you?" Levi asked.

"Levi!" I exclaimed as I slapped him on the shoulder.

"What?" He played innocent. That didn't work with me anymore.

"As a matter of fact, he does," Thistle finally spoke.

"And he's very good at it," Briar said with a purr.

"That's hilarious," Aydan said. "I get it. Rape and pillage."

"Christ on a cracker! Levi, get up there and get that pirate pixie out of my attic," I demanded.

"Yes, ma'am," he laughed, and climbed up the stairs to save Pirate Bramble from the scratcher in the attic.

~

"SQUIRREL," Levi said.

"You sure?" I asked, as I dried my hair with a towel.

"Yep," he replied. "Hey, do you know why a squirrel swims on his back?"

"Levi," I groaned.

"He's keeping his nuts dry," he said, laughing at his own lame joke.

"That's terrible." I smiled, because I liked corny jokes and he knew it.

"Why are you laughing?" he asked.

"I'm not laughing. You are laughing," I replied.

"I didn't think it was funny," Winnie said from the kitchen table. She was smiling widely. She adored Levi from the start, and he could do no wrong by her. She and I had our conflicts, but I chalked it up to being a typical mother/daughter relationship. At the end of the day, I loved her with all my heart. And she loved Levi. I tried not to be jealous.

"Here you are, Miss Not Laughing," I said setting a bowl of cereal in front of her. "Luther will be here soon, so eat up."

"Mom?"

"Yes?"

"Do you think that I was sick because I have some of you in me?" she asked.

"Absolutely," Levi said.

"I am going to…"

"Please. Please do it," he begged playfully.

"Shut up," I said, cutting him off. "Winnie, I don't know why you were sick. I'm just glad you are better."

"Sometimes I feel cold," she said.

"Cold?" She shouldn't feel cold at all. She was a phoenix. I placed my hand on her forehead and the familiar warmth of her father rushed over me. Whenever I touched Winnie, I felt Dylan. Levi eyed me as I removed my hand. He never said it bothered him, but he knew what I was feeling. "You feel normal to me."

4

"Just sometimes," she said.

"When you do, will you tell me?" I asked.

"Okay," she replied.

Aydan and Callum came barrelling through the kitchen. "Bye, Mom," Aydan said, kissing me on the cheek.

"Where are you going? You've been out all night!" I protested. The keys to his father's Camaro jingled in his hand.

"Bye, Mom," Callum said, kissing me on the other cheek. I didn't know why he had taken to calling me Mom, but I didn't complain. I might as well have a whole house of adopted children.

"*I am not your child,*" Levi said. "*So, don't expect any good-bye kisses from me.*"

"*Thank you for the clarification,*" I replied. He grinned, and I started itching to jerk that knot.

"We are going to help Tennyson. He's working with Michael Handley today on weapons," Callum explained. Michael and his father were blacksmiths, forgers, and welders. Tennyson insisted that this war would be fought in the old ways. Swords, arrows, and shields. We were equipping every day for battle. The battle to take back my father's realm. Winter.

And now my children were involved, and it scared the shit out of me.

"Be safe. I love you," I said, watching them head out the door to the garage.

"Love you, too," they called back to me.

Levi stepped into my gaze at the door and placed his hand on my neck. "Get dressed. We have a progress meeting this morning."

I sighed and nodded. He leaned over and kissed me on the lips. I felt Winnie's eyes on us. It always made me nervous. Levi laughed at me, removing his hand from my neck.

"You smell like griffin," I said.

"Well, I had to wrestle one of the bastards," he said.

"We need a griffin law," I said.

"The town council really doesn't meet anymore. It's all war stuff," Levi said. "I think the griffins will be better this time. Aydan laid down the law."

5

"Oh really?"

"I'll tell you about it on the way. Go get a shower," he said.

"What about you?" I asked.

"I'll get one as soon as Luther gets here to get Winnie," he replied.

Was it bad that I'd rather he'd just shower with me? I knew he wouldn't do it. Levi had this romanticized notion that our first time should be memorable. No quickies. It didn't make me any less horny.

CHAPTER TWO

After taking showers and Luther picking up Winnie, Levi and I made our way to the office. In front of the new trailer park, our office sat surrounded by vehicles and people from in the town.

"What is going on?" I asked.

"I dunno. We are going to have to park on the street," Levi said, pulling over on the main road. "Looks like they are having a clearance on Yeti cups at the sporting goods store."

"What kind of cups?"

"Yeti cups," Levi said. "They keep ice forever."

"Hmm. Never had a problem with that," I grinned.

"You gotta do something about this, Grace!" Mrs. Frist yelled at me.

"About what?" I asked.

"The invasion," Lamar added.

"Invasion?" Levi asked.

"I found one in my makeup drawer. He'd chewed my best highlighter!" Chaz whined. "I'm devastated!"

Levi moved closer to me, escorting me through the angry townspeople to the deck of our trailer.

"I've got my shotgun ready!" Cletus called out waving the gun over his head.

"Alright, now! Everyone calm down," Levi called out to them. The raging crowd quietened to a murmur. His magic was subtle as it brushed over them. I felt it, but it was light and unnoticeable for the most part.

Henrietta Purcell with her plump, pink cheeks stepped forward with a snarl in her tusk. "This town has been overrun by these vile creatures. You must do something about it."

"What creatures?" I asked.

"Bushy-tailed bastards," Lamar shouted, followed by a chorus of affirmation from the rest of the crowd.

"Squirrels?" Levi asked.

"Yes! They are everywhere. In all the houses, scratching all night long. It's an omen!" Mrs. Frist fretted.

"I can't believe we are pitchin' a hissy fit about squirrels," I muttered.

"I can go get Bramble," Levi whispered back.

I giggled. "Maybe not," I said. "Alright. I'm sure there is an explanation. Levi and I will look into it. In the meantime, go home and put some food outside for them, so they will get out of your homes."

"They attacked my storeroom," Juanita Santiago said. Mrs. Santiago ran the biggest farm in Shady Grove with the help of Deacon Giles and the Yule Lads.

"How bad is it?" Levi asked. Her storeroom had been built beneath the ground to store the large amounts of produce that the farm yielded. It was a huge source of food for the whole town.

"Deacon is there picking through it now. There were about twenty of them there," she said.

"What are we going to eat?" someone exclaimed from the back.

"We will provide whatever you need. Tennyson and Levi will tap our resources beyond the wards of the town. Don't you worry your pretty little heads. We've got this," I assured them with a syrupy sweet tone. Mrs. Sharolyn always used to say that you catch more bees with honey than vinegar.

"She's right. We have nothing to be overly concerned about with these squirrels. For all we know, they are just storing up for a cold spell," Levi added.

I felt magical movement in the trailer behind us. At least one of my knights had arrived, sensing our tenseness from the conversation with the citizens. Astor stepped out on the porch behind us with Ella in tow. They looked frazzled but stood behind us in support. Ella's belly stretched out ahead of herself like a basketball on the edge of a rim.

Then I felt them. Both of them. Ignoring the crowd, I walked over and placed my hand on her belly.

"What is it?" she asked quietly.

"They are fine," I said with a smile.

"They?" she asked.

"What?!" Astor gulped.

"Two. There are two. I feel them both," I said. Levi had turned from the crowd which had grown quiet.

"Twins," she smiled.

"Yes," I grinned.

A loud thud shook the porch as Astor's body hit it like a ton of concrete blocks. "Astor!" Ella cried out, as we rushed to his motionless body. Levi started to giggle as Ella tapped his face. "Wake up, Astor."

"He's taking it well," Levi laughed. He stood up to talk the crowd as Tabitha and Remy pushed through it to get to Astor. "Y'all go home. I'll send word when we hear something. We will deal with your needs individually. Contact Troy and the wolves with any issues."

As the crowd dispersed, Tab reached out to pull open Astor's eyelids. "He's out cold," she said.

"I can wake him," I said.

"No," Levi said quickly.

"I won't hurt him," I protested.

"No, but you would definitely have some sort of evil enjoyment from it," he returned.

"Really? Me? Evil?" I asked.

"Um, yeah," he replied.

"I agree with him," Remy said behind me.

"I'm gonna knock you into next week, Remington Blake. No one asked you," I said.

"Thanks for the back-up, Remy. It's nice to know I'm not the only one that's had to deal with her," Levi continued.

"I swear to the goddess, I am going to…"

"What? You are going to, what?" Levi asked.

I growled at him, and everyone on the porch laughed. Astor began to shake off the shock and wake up.

"Oh, shit, that hurt," he groaned. I backed away from them crossing my arms. Fucking Levi always knew how to shut me down. That's fine. I would fix his little red wagon. Or rather I wouldn't. Not until he apologized.

"Here," Levi said giving him a hand. Remy took his other, and they hauled the big ginger knight off the deck.

"Are you sure, Grace?" Astor asked.

I nodded in response.

"*Quit pouting*," Levi said.

I ignored him which he was prepared for as a response. He lifted an eyebrow and shook his head. So much emotion in his denim blue eyes. Frustration, humor, love. His beard had filled in nicely, and he kept it trimmed and neat. He looked so much older with it, which was why I expected he had grown it out.

"I can double check, but she is probably right," Tabitha said. "As the ruler of this realm, she knows her subjects better than I do."

"Don't feed her ego, my dear," Remy said with a wink to me.

"It can't get any bigger," Tab replied.

They were all teasing, but I had had enough. My skin was wearing a little thin. Levi walked up to me, wrapping his arms around my waist. He folded his hands at my lower back, forcing my body to his.

"I'm sorry," he whispered.

"No, you aren't. Let me go," I said, wiggling away from him.

"Why are you always trying to get away from me?" he asked. That twinkle in his eye meant he was just teasing me.

"I'm not," I said. He leaned over and placed a kiss on the tip of my nose.

"You look madder than a snake that realized his mate was a garden hose," he said.

"At least he's getting some," I muttered.

He leaned into my ear, and his breath moved my hair. Tingles rolled down my body from the crown of my head to the tips of my toes. "Soon," he whispered.

That horny fairy inside of me started jerking around in her straight jacket. Crazy, little wench. "Not soon enough," I said.

He stepped toward me pushing me to the railing of the porch. "Excuse me?" he asked.

"Levi," I hissed, looking over his shoulder. Our friends were purposefully not looking at us, but I could see the grins on their faces. Levi huffed a light laugh, then turned to them.

"Congratulations, Fire Crotch. Well done!" Levi exclaimed, patting Astor on the back.

"Two! What am I going to do with two?!" Astor tittered.

Tab and Ella were giggling and holding her swelling belly. Remy watched them as they went into the trailer. His eyes met mine, and for a moment, I saw that handsome devil that I used to love. Another time and another place it would have been right for us. We both knew it. I was just glad that we had managed a friendship out of it in the end.

"Isn't about time you and Tab got hitched?" I asked.

"Nah. We are good," Remy said.

"Babies?" I asked.

"Hell, naw. What would I do with a mess of youngins?" he scoffed.

"Be a good Dad," I replied.

He stopped for a moment and his eyes twinkled. "Thank you, Gracie. That means a lot."

"You are welcome," I replied.

"You comin'?" Levi said, offering me his hand.

I looked at it and huffed. I walked into the trailer past both of them as they laughed.

Astor sat next to Ella on the couch in my office rubbing her belly. He talked softly to it. It seemed kinda silly, but he didn't care what any of us thought. I sat behind my desk as Levi sat on the front edge.

"The squirrels are everywhere," Tabitha said.

"Summer?" I asked.

"It's possible," she said.

"I think it's time for a blizzard," I said.

"What do you mean?" Ella asked.

"The critters will hide out if I turn down the temperature," I said. "They might even leave town, if it gets frigid enough."

"We can't do that until we get supplies into town," Levi said. "Tennyson is on his way."

"Where is Troy?" I asked.

"Amanda is pregnant, too," Ella said.

"What?" I asked.

"I don't think they were ready to tell everyone," Astor muttered.

"Oops!" Ella said. "I'll blame it on pregnancy hormones."

Tennyson trudged in with Aydan and Callum. "What has gotten everyone in a tizzy?"

"Squirrel invasion," Astor said.

"And Astor's having twins," I added.

Tennyson grinned, slapping Astor on the shoulder. "Well done!"

"He fainted," Levi said.

"I did not faint, Bard! I stumbled and fell," Astor protested.

"You are a sure-footed knight capable of meeting any foe in battle with a sword. Surely, you did not fall!" Tennyson laughed.

Astor blushed, turning back to the mother of his unborn children. She cupped his cheek with her hand and whispered something sweet. He placed a soft kiss on her hand before she withdrew.

If I ever needed a reminder of the purpose of our fight, that little exchange was it. Good friends sharing in a celebratory jest and a tender moment of love. My resolve hardened each time I witnessed these moments between my friends and family.

Aydan and Callum stood quietly against the wall of the room watching as everyone gushed over the Knight's twins.

"*Did you know about Amanda?*" I asked Levi.

"*No, but I think having children has been a point of contention between them,*" Levi said.

"*I wonder why?*" I asked.

"*Troy didn't want to have kids. They have Mark,*" Levi said.

"*Do you agree with him?*" I asked.

"*Not my place to agree or disagree, but I know he's been grumpy lately. Now I know why,*" he said.

"*You haven't mentioned that he was grumpy,*" I pushed.

He looked from our friends to my eyes. "*Guys don't talk about those kinds of things. Besides if I thought it was anything more than a family matter, I would have told you.*"

I looked down at the desk, breaking his stare. "*I didn't mean anything by it,*" I said.

"*I know,*" he replied. "So, squirrels. I mean, seriously, are we having this conversation?"

"I haven't noticed any squirrels," Tennyson said.

"They avoid your foul demeanor," I said. He scowled at me.

"If we are going to blizzard the place, we'll need to bring in supplies. Plus, they have already hit the Santiago food storage," Levi said, bringing us all back to the reality of the situation. No matter how much a farce it seemed to be, anything could happen in Shady Grove.

The planning commenced. Tennyson and Levi handled all the particulars involving bringing in food supplies. Astor made suggestions, while Ella and Tab talked quietly about the needs of the children in town. If it was going to get cold, and that seemed to be the prevailing course of action, we would need winter gear which was not something easily found in the perpetually hot state of Alabama. We had 90-degree days in the middle of winter. This winter itself had been particularly rainy. Rain or shine, it didn't matter. I could make it snow.

"Have you decided what to do with her?" Tennyson asked, referring to Stephanie, who had been our prisoner now for almost three months. I had hoped to get information from her about Brockton's plans, but it didn't matter what we did to her. She didn't tell us shit.

"She talking?" I asked.

"No. Jenny visits at least once a week, but Stephanie isn't budging," he reported.

"I cannot go against the original sentence. She betrayed us all," I said. Earlier in the week, I had talked to Joey Blankenship about the possibility that Devin might lose his mother. He assured me that his son wanted nothing to do with her, but I knew that one day, he might. One day, he might wonder why we executed her. The Santiago children were already without a parent. I was facing the possibility of killing another parent.

With everything she had done to Dylan and to me, I should have been itching to dust her, but part of me loathed the idea. Executions were nasty business. Killing a mother amped up my concerns.

"*I'll do it,*" Levi said.

"*It's my responsibility,*" I said.

"*This partnership was your idea. So, share the responsibilities,*" he said.

"Stop being so assertive," I said. The room got quiet. Tennyson grinned. "Don't you smile! It's your fault that he's like this."

"Actually, it was already there, I just encouraged it," Tennyson replied. "Stephanie can rot in jail for a little while longer. She's not going anywhere."

"I can promise that," Troy said as he entered the room.

"Hey! Everything okay?" I asked.

"Just spending the afternoon treeing squirrels," he said. He was serious.

"Good grief," I muttered.

"What we need is a good critter catcher," Remy said. "I'll make some calls."

"You know critter catchers?" I asked.

"I know everyone," he replied with an eyebrow waggle.

The meeting broke up. One by one our friends left the room, but Troy stayed behind. He was ready to tell us what we already knew. He sat down on the couch after shaking Tennyson's hand.

The strings on Levi's tattoo ignited into sound, surrounding the room in a silencing barrier.

"How did you know I needed that?" Troy asked. Levi sat down on the couch with him.

"Ella let it slip," Levi said.

He buried his head in his hands. "Damn. I guess Amanda told her," he groaned.

"I thought babies were a good thing," I said.

"We are going to war, Grace. I'm bringing children into the world during a war!" he exclaimed.

"Well, I mean there are ways to prevent pregnancy," I said.

"Grace, not helping," Levi scolded. I shrugged.

"The problem is we had decided to wait, but she missed a pill or two and didn't tell me," he said. I found it curious that even werewolves had to take birth control.

"Troy, you are blessed, and you will be a great father," I said. "Dylan would have agreed with me."

He shook his head. "My line has always been troublesome. I've not talked about it, but my father's pack were roamers. We didn't have a territory. We moved from place to place taking what we could from other packs. I refused to participate in it anymore which was why I left. It was how I ended up here. I never wanted to spread that bloodline to a child. We have Mark. He is my son," Troy huffed.

"Man, life has a way of throwing us curveballs. This isn't the end of the world. Your children will follow you, and you are one of the best men I have ever known. Grace is right. Children are a blessing. We will protect them as fiercely as we do our own," Levi said.

Our own. I knew Levi loved my kids, but to hear him claim them made my internal fairy pop a buckle on that straight jacket that I tried to keep on her.

"Thank you, Levi. It's going to be okay. But it won't be long before they are here. We need a few things," he said.

"We will get them," I said.

"Yes, we will," Levi echoed.

CHAPTER THREE

SILENCE WAS RARE AROUND OUR HOUSE, BUT WHEN LEVI AND I walked in from the meeting, we were alone. I intended to make a smart remark, but his lips were on mine before I could. From that first kiss in the parking lot at the Food Mart, I knew Levi had skills, but I had no idea how good he was. I attributed it to his love talker heritage. There was no way in this world he was just a natural talent. I shoved him down on the couch and straddled his lap.

One surprise to me was that once his lips started working, he stopped talking. No smart remarks. No silly jokes. Just lips and tongue. And moans. Sometimes I wasn't sure whether it was me or him.

Dragging my lips from his, I hovered over his face while he looked up at me. My blonde hair cascaded around us. He worked his hands under my shirt and up my back, kneading muscle with each movement.

The kids would be here at any moment, and I knew this wasn't our time. I craved him more than I ever expected. Once I allowed myself to consider it, I knew, there would never be anyone else for me, but him. Why prolong it? Why wait? Levi was mine the moment he walked into my trailer with Jeremiah.

"Gloriana," he whispered. "You are the most exquisite being I have ever seen." He pushed his palms in my back pressing me closer to him. With his lips, he kissed his way up my neck to my ear. "You are finally mine."

"All yours," I smiled.

Before our lips touched again, the rumble of a V8 engine approached the house. The boys were home. I slumped down on Levi and rocked my hips two or three times.

"I say we adopt them all out."

He laughed but clamped his hands down on my hips. "Stop rocking."

I rocked again.

"Damn it, Grace," he groaned.

"You started this," I said with another rock. "Besides, it's not me that wants it to be *special*." His face wrinkled up with frustration, then he realized that I'd said it on purpose to make him brood. He tried to smile, but the brood pushed its way through.

Car doors banged in the garage. With a swift move, Levi tossed me up off of him and ran up the stairs.

"You can run, but you can't hide!" I screamed at his retreat.

"Hey mom," Aydan said.

"Aydan! Did you guys have a good day?" I asked.

"I guess," Callum said, making his way to the fridge. "Did you know that Troy and Amanda were pregnant?"

"I did," I replied.

"That's crazy," Callum said.

"Why is it crazy?" I asked.

"The pack just assumed that Mark would be the next alpha, but Amanda isn't giving up any information about his father. I'm not even sure Troy knows who the father was. Anyway, now that they are going to have kids, one of them will be alpha."

"Wait? Why? But Troy adopted Mark," I said.

"That's true, but wolf politics isn't like fairy politics. I know Winnie is your daughter. Dylan's daughter by adoption. The power passed to her, but with the wolves it's different. Mark would have to show some sign of developing into an alpha, but he hasn't. He probably doesn't have the bloodline," Callum explained as he rummaged through the fridge.

"For someone who isn't quite a wolf, you seem to know a lot about it," I said.

"Mom," Aydan scolded.

"No, it's fine. She's right. I'm not a wolf like they are. I'm more like you," Callum said to Aydan who lowered his head as he took a can of coke from Callum. I ruffled his hair, catching the scent of leather and mint like his father. It made me think of the jacket. I should really give it to Aydan.

"I didn't mean anything by it. Besides, I don't care what you are. You are family to me now," I said.

"I know, Mom," he smiled.

"How does a wolf exhibit alpha tendencies?" I asked. "He's very protective of Winnie."

"It's not just protection. It's leadership and provision. Mark has learned to work with the wolves in scouting parties, but he's never stepped up to lead a group. Troy has given him the opportunity."

"He's just a child," I said.

"He's a wolf," Callum rebutted.

"I see," I replied.

"Where is Winnie?" Aydan asked.

"She was with Luther today. They should be back soon," I said.

"Did we interrupt you and Uncle Levi?" Aydan asked.

"No," I said, blushing.

"We did," Callum teased.

"No. We knew you guys would be home soon," I said.

"Mom, are you going to marry him?" Aydan asked.

"We haven't talked about it," I said. I wanted to add that we hadn't gotten past second base because of the craziness in this town, but I figured I'd leave that part out.

"I know about Dad's dream," he said.

"That damn dream," I grumbled. "Look. I love Levi. I never imagined I would. I never thought I'd love anyone but your father, and loving Levi doesn't make me forget Dylan."

"I'm not offended," Aydan said. Callum watched us have the

conversation without interrupting. "If he ever did anything to hurt you though, I would kill him."

"You could try," Levi said coming back down the stairs.

"I'm serious, Uncle Levi," Aydan said.

"I know you are," Levi replied. "But I'd rather pluck my own eyes out than hurt your mom."

"He's just a little emotional today it seems," I said. Occasionally, Aydan did have moments where he was a child in a grown-up body. Most of the time, it was evident in his emotions.

"He's right to protect you," Levi said. *"I'm proud of him for saying it."*

"I'd help him," Callum added.

"I could take both of you," Levi replied.

"Oh, really?" Aydan said.

"I could. No magic," Levi boasted.

"Oh, please," I groaned, as the dicks were waved around the room.

"Maybe we could fight it out at Troy's," Aydan suggested.

"Troy shut down the fights after our trip to the Otherworld," Levi said.

"Just an excuse, Uncle Levi. You are scared. It's okay to admit it. Mom will still love you," Aydan teased.

They went back and forth for a while until the next thing I knew they were all arm wrestling on the dining room table. Thankfully, Winnie came home to dilute the testosterone in the room.

"What are they doing?" she asked after she gave me a hug.

"Being men," I replied.

"Looks stupid," she said.

"Out of the mouth of babes," I laughed. "How was your day?"

"It was fun. Luther's granddaughter is here. She's a genie," she said.

"A jinn," I corrected. I'd known a few jinn in my lifetime, and they hated the term genie.

"Yes! She's awesome. We are the same age, and we played outside," Winnie gushed.

"What's her name?" I asked.

"Soraya. Luther said she is named after the stars," Winnie said. "I'm named after a star too."

I laughed, and I saw Levi crack a smile across the room as Aydan and Callum matched up. Their arms flexed, and they grunted loudly. I was surprised that Aydan held his own with Callum. I would have thought the older boy would have had more strength.

"Yes, you are. A different kind of star, but you are unique and special," I said.

Her face turned darker. "Mark was there, too," she said.

"Did he follow you there?" I asked.

"No, Luther lets him help me with target practice," she said, lifting her hand to form a small fireball above it. My insides lurched looking at the flaring magic. The arm-wrestling match stopped, and we stared at Winnie. "Relax. I got it."

"You sure?" I asked.

"Yep. I'm doing better," she said.

Suddenly, the fire wobbled, and Winnie's face constricted as she focused on the flame. The ball turned a deep blue color like the hottest flame, then burst into ice particles which fell around her hand like snow.

"Are you okay?" I asked in a panic. Levi rushed across the room to us with the boys right behind him.

"That happens sometimes. Luther said my winter is getting in the way," Winnie huffed. "Why can't I just do fire and not both?"

"I didn't know you could do winter," I said.

"I'm not trying to do it. You didn't change it to ice?" she asked me.

"No, baby, I didn't," I said.

"It's okay, Winnie. You are doing a great job," Levi said, encouraging her.

"You think?" she asked with wide green eyes. Levi froze looking at her with his mouth hanging open.

"Green eyes," Levi rasped.

I grabbed her cheeks turning her to me to look at her face. "Your eyes are green," I said.

"My eyes are brown," she said.

Looking up to Levi, I questioned him without saying a word. He shrugged in response. I pulled Winnie into a tight hug. "You are doing a wonderful job, Winnie. I am so proud."

"Thank you, Momma," she said, hugging me back.

CHAPTER FOUR

THE SPARKLES SWIRLED AROUND IN MY COFFEE CUP AS NESTOR finished up his chores. I loved my grandfather and he tended to give the best advice in town. I'd come down to Hot Tin Roof to pick his brain. Levi and Tennyson were on a supply run, and Winnie insisted on being dropped off at the Diner to play with Soraya. Callum and Aydan had run off early in the morning and I hadn't heard from them.

"Squirrels?"

"You haven't had any problems?" I asked.

"No, thank goodness. The damn things can be annoying though," he said.

"There was one in our attic, but it seems that pirate Bramble ran it off," I said.

"I don't even want to know," he laughed.

"No, you don't," I confirmed.

"And Winnie has a new friend," he said.

"And winter powers," I added.

"You don't say. I wonder where that came from," he said, giving me the eye.

"Did you suspect that she would get winter fairy powers?" I asked.

"I knew it was a possibility when you gave her the fruit from the tree and water from the fountain. You made her a fairy. She gets it from you. She's more your daughter now than she ever has been. I think it's fitting though. Dylan got to give her the fire. You give her the ice," he said.

"It's two competing powers and that much harder for her to learn to control it," I huffed.

"She will get it," he said with full confidence.

"How's my great grandson?" he asked.

"Aydan and Callum are inseparable, except when Callum visits the wolves," I said. "Then he's momma's boy." I loved thinking about the few times that Aydan and I have had together. We often walked out to the stone circle, talking about life. It's amazing how quickly his mind and body adapted to his age change. He had a sweetness about him that I was sure that he didn't get from me. Dylan had his moments, but he wasn't as darling as my son could be. It was nice to see that he would make his own mark on the world without either of us influencing it.

"He's a good kid. He's been around here helping me some," Nestor said. "Callum helps too. Mostly with moving things around and cleaning up."

"Good. I'm happy to hear they have picked a worthy cause," I said.

"Cleaning the bar?" Nestor asked.

"No, helping their grandfather," I replied. He knew what I meant.

"How are things with you and Levi?" he asked.

"Fine," I replied.

"Not fine?" he asked.

"No, just frustrated," I said.

"Say no more. I don't need to know," he said.

"Well, it's just that we've delayed the inevitable for so long that now it doesn't seem so inevitable," I sighed.

Nestor laughed, "That's what you get for teasing him for so long."

"What? I did not tease him," I protested.

"You did, and he took it. He loved every minute of it. Just like Dylan," he said. "They are more alike than you realize."

"No, Levi has his own place, and puts me in mine," I said.

"Good for him," Nestor said.

"Whose side are you on?" I asked.

"Yours. Always yours," he smiled. "How about the war prep?"

"Going well, I guess. Tennyson said that by spring we should have the weapons we need. His guys are training as many in town that are willing, on a daily basis," I said. "I'm sure Brock knows everything that is going on though. He will be ready."

"That realm is yours by right. You will take it," Nestor said.

"At what cost?" I asked.

"If you don't, the cost will be the entire world." It was staggering to think that one ruler held the reins to the world above and below. "We all know the price will be high. It will be worth it. Which reminds me, Mike was in yesterday. I think he's got some new concoctions for you."

"Cool. I always enjoy visiting with Mike," I said. "What if we win, Ness?"

"What do you mean?" He stopped wiping glasses and stared at me.

"How do I rule here and there? I don't want to live in Winter," I said.

"It will all work out, Gracie. Don't worry," he said with a smile. I almost believed that it would work out, but there were so many loose ends to tie up.

"What do I do with Stephanie?" I asked.

"She's to be executed, right?" he asked. "If you let her live, she will continue to do harm to you. Perhaps even to your children."

I grimaced. He was right. I don't know why I had been beating around the bush. I needed to talk to Levi and just go do it. It was time for Stephanie to cease to live.

25

The door opened behind us. I turned to see my favorite wolf outside of Callum. "Howdy, Nick," I said.

"Hey, Grace," he said, planting a kiss on my cheek. "I'll get one in while the bard isn't here."

Nestor and I laughed at him.

"Coffee?"

"Yes, please. It's turning cold outside. Are you doing that?" he asked me.

"Not yet. As soon as we get the supplies in though, we might have snow. Just to run off the squirrels," I said.

"One of those damn things ate a hole in the seat on my bike," he groaned.

"Bike?" I asked.

"Yeah, I have a motorcycle," he said. "Took a little while to get used to it again." He held up his handless arm. I winced at it because it was my fault he was missing the hand. He still hadn't shifted since it happened. However, he swore that everything was fine with the pack. They had accepted him back as family.

"I'm sorry," I muttered.

"Grace, I've told you a thousand times, and I'll tell you a thousand more, I would not have changed a thing. Besides, you are working on that regrowth spell," he smiled.

"I think you have me confused with Levi," I said.

"Maybe so," he grinned. Levi had been working on finding a spell, but we hadn't come up with anything yet. He even looked through Mable's old book hoping we could find something. I had asked Mike to look into some regrowth potions. Perhaps that is what he wanted to talk about with me.

"What about your fairy side?" I asked.

"What about it?" He took a sip of Nestor's coffee. I watched as his face morphed into a calm serenity. He had let his hair grow out, and it had gotten pretty shaggy. He wore jeans with a rip in the knee and a leather jacket over a white t-shirt. He had a bad boy, James Dean thing going on.

"Can't you just glamour the hand?" I asked.

"I was never any good at glamours. When I could get one to

work, it would fade too quickly to be functional," he explained. "Unless you know some tricks."

"I know lots of tricks."

"Don't flirt with me, Grace Ann Bryant. You will get us both in trouble," he said, taking another sip of the coffee.

Dominick had become one of my favorite people, and I didn't have an ounce of attraction for him in the sexual way. He was definitely handsome in a roguish way, but my heart belonged to another. My affections for Nick had absolutely nothing to do with the fact that he sacrificed his hand to save my life. It had to do with the fact he was a good guy with a good sense of humor, and I trusted him with my life and the life of my children.

The door to the bar opened again, and we were joined by my fair-haired brother.

"Oh! Just wait until I tell Levi that I caught the two of you," Finley teased.

"Go ahead. Tell him," I replied.

"Hey, Glory," he said, giving me a kiss on the cheek just like Dominick had done.

"Glory," Dominick repeated.

"Don't even," I warned him.

"I like it," he said. Finley laughed.

"Hush!" I scolded him. Nestor sat a cup of coffee down for Finley.

"How's Riley?" Nick asked. I was glad he asked, so I didn't have to bring it up.

"She's fine. She spends a lot of time with Wendy and Kady," he replied. "Have you given in to Levi yet?"

Dominick choked on his coffee, and Nestor laughed.

"I hate all of you," I sassed.

"No, you don't," Finley said. "But really? Please tell me that you have."

"It's none of your business," I insisted.

"Poor Levi," Finley said.

Dominick looked away from me because he was laughing.

"You want me to call him right now and do it?" I asked.

27

"Sure. I dare you," Finley teased. This was the brother I remembered. I was happy to have him back, even if he was giving me hell. Perhaps Riley was good for him after all.

"Levi!" I shouted. They all looked at me in shock.

"I was joking, Glory. Geez," Finley said.

Levi appeared in the room as ordered.

"You know you don't have to come every time she calls," Finley insisted.

"Yeah, I'm sure that would work out well for me," Levi said. "What's going on?"

Nestor sat another cup of coffee on the counter for Levi. Dominick got up and moved over a stool, so Levi could sit next to me. Levi leaned over to kiss me on the cheek, but he stopped. Somehow, he could sense that both Nick and Finley had kissed my cheek. I shook my head so he would know that I was on to him.

"Tell him," I said to Finley.

"Um, well." Finley fumbled his words. "I didn't know she was going to summon you."

I smiled at him, and he took the opportunity to kiss me lightly on the lips.

"It's none of your business, Finley," Levi said.

Bravo. We hadn't shared a private word, but he knew exactly what Finley had done to rile me up.

"My bad," Finley said.

With a tinkling shimmer in the room, Luther and Zahir arrived.

"Good to see you, Zahir," I said greeting him.

"You as well, my Queen," he said with a bow of his head.

"Betty and I have locked down the diner. We will keep it closed for the duration of the snow," Luther said. "She's taking Winnie home with her. You can pick her up later."

"What brings you to town?" I asked Zahir.

"Soraya," he said.

"Luther's granddaughter. Winnie seems quite taken with her," I said. "Something about BFFs."

"Soraya can touch the realm where Zahir resides," Luther explained. "She, like Winnie, is just learning to use her gifts."

"Interesting," I said, as the two men took seats at the bar. Nestor provided coffee for each of them.

A large circle of light ignited near the pool table. Astor and Tennyson stepped through holding their swords. I moved to the edge of my seat thinking there might be a problem that I hadn't sensed, but Tennyson waved his hand.

"We are just here for coffee," Astor said, looking haggard.

"Astor, you look like ten miles of bad road," Levi commented.

"Pregnancy hormones suck," he grumbled.

"Tell me about it," Troy said at the door of the bar.

"Well, if it isn't all my knights at once," I exclaimed. "No round table needed. Just a bar and good coffee. Join us, Troy."

"I think I will," Troy said, taking a seat next to Finley. Nestor poured two cups of coffee. He gave one to Troy, then sat down on a stool behind the counter with his cup.

"Are we ready for this?" I asked.

"Yes," Tennyson replied immediately.

"We are, Grace," Levi insisted.

"Heavy snow or blizzard?" I asked.

"I think heavy snow will do it," Astor replied.

"Boring," I teased. "Sound the alarm. We will give the town time to get ready while we finish our coffee."

Nestor sat down his cup, picked up the phone on the wall, and began spreading the word. It was about to snow in Shady Grove.

CHAPTER FIVE

NESTOR FINISHED CALLING OUR CONTACTS ACROSS TOWN TO LET them know that the snow was coming. We sat and teased Astor about fainting, and encouraged Troy who still seemed out sorts.

"So, I'm an official knight now?" Dominick asked.

"It's your choice. Everyone here has sworn their allegiance to me," I said.

"I'm pretty sure I sacrificed a hand to prove my allegiance," he joked.

"We swore blood oaths to her," Levi interjected.

"Wow. I didn't think such a thing still existed," Dominick said. "Tell me what to do, and I'll do it."

Tennyson held out a small knife. "Your blood is my blood. I swear my fealty to you," Tennyson said, repeating the oath he had once given to me.

Dominick dragged his palm across the knife. Then, he knelt before me. "I am Dominick Meyer, disowned son of my father, forgotten son of my mother."

"Stop," I said.

"What? I can't state who I am without the truth," Nick said.

"You are my Beta," Troy growled. "The past no longer matters."

This was more than just an oath to me. This was the moment that Dominick needed to know that his family had changed. I would never disown him or forget him. Nor would any of those present.

"Right," he said, clearing his throat. "I am Dominick Meyer, Beta of the Shady Grove Pack, your blood is my blood. I swear my fealty to you," he said, offering his hand to me. Taking the knife from Tennyson, I used it to slice open my own palm.

"Dominick Meyer, I accept your oath as given." Clasping his hand with mine. His blood mingled with mine. I felt the fairy tingle that still lived inside of him, even if he didn't use it. He still had power. A power that he would need in the future. "Now you are mine!"

The men in the room laughed. Dominick rose, looking at the room around him. "We are your brothers now," Levi said, offering his hand.

Dominick shook it. I saw the glittering of tears swimming in his eyes even though he was determined not to release them.

"Welcome to the family," I said, giving him a big hug. "Now, it's time for snow!"

Levi followed me closely as I went into the parking lot in front of the Hot Tin Roof. Thankfully, it was already cloudy. Reaching deep within the earth, I closed my eyes and pulled on the power of Winter along with the water and wind stones. When I opened my eyes, Levi stood in front of me.

"Unleash it all. I'm here, and I won't let you go too far," he said, as he had so many times before when I feared using my coldest powers. The wind picked up as we stood there.

"I don't fear it like I used to because I know you are here," I said.

"I'll always be here," he said.

"That's not a promise you can keep," I said.

"Yes, it is. I swear by it."

Winter power felt cold and unruly to me. Beyond the edges of the Winter realm was where the wild fairies lived, and I had always believed those wild things were just part of us, making Winter power unruly. But now, with that power swirling inside of me, I felt control like I never had. Levi's confidence and steadfast support solidified my authority over the wild.

"I love you, Levi," I said.

"I know you do," he laughed.

"I'm trying to have a moment here!" I protested.

"No, you are just realizing how important I am to you. I mean, I've always known it, but it's cool that you have come to grips with the truth," he teased. "Now, make it snow."

I hated that he always found a way to say things in a way that I couldn't respond. That way, he got the last word. The generic tail-knot comment didn't seem to fit.

Instead, I did as he suggested. Lifting my arms high into the air, I pushed the winter cold into the boiling clouds overhead. They grew to giant fluffy marshmallows, then unleashed heavy precipitation down on the earth. Snow fell silently around us in heavy clumps quickly covering the grass and trees.

I felt Levi's hand caress my throat. "This is it. The part of you I love the most. Your true self." How many times had I heard him say that in my head since that day on his motorcycle in the woods?

"The deadly cold power that could snuff out any life in this town. Yeah, I'm awesome." I belittled myself.

"If you meant that, I would slap you," he grinned.

"You could try."

"I love the heart pounding in your chest with fairy power. I can hear its beat like the undercurrent of a ballad. That ballad is our story. You and me. Together we are a perfect song," he said.

"I've been barded," I quipped.

"Not yet, you haven't," he returned. He followed it with a light kiss as the snow fell around us. The kiss deepened to a pulsing desire. His tattoo ignited in the storm, playing a song I'd never heard. A pounding beat over a glorious melody. My heart and his song. It sank into my soul, filling a hole that I didn't know I had. The song slowed, and he pulled his lips from mine.

"Wow," I gasped.

"I love you, too."

WE REMAINED at the bar for a time with the knights taking in reports from across the town. The squirrels seemed to have ceased their assault. The children were enjoying the snow, and Tennyson confirmed that the storm remained inside the wards surrounding the town. It seemed like an overall success. I should have known it was too easy.

"Hello," Nestor said answering the old corded phone which still hung on the wall in the bar. He listened to the voice on the other end. "I see. They are here. I will tell them." He hung up the phone.

"What is it?" I asked.

"Deacon needs you to come out to the farm," he said.

"More squirrels?" I asked.

"Nope. This is much bigger," Nestor replied.

TROY and I stepped through a portal made by Levi's sword. He followed after closing the portal. We stood in a foot of snow outside Deacon Giles farmhouse. I was alarmed to see him standing on the porch. Instead of the lowly farmer, Krampus stood there with his blackened eyes, sharp teeth, and one horn. He waved us toward him.

"*It doesn't matter how many times I see him like that, he's creepy as fuck,*" I said to Levi.

"*Something has spooked him if he transformed. Stay alert,*" he warned.

I nodded. Troy held one hand to his side with his thumb running over one half of Driggs. The other half sat on his other hip. He preferred the fire to the lightning, so I was sure that it was the flaming gun that he wore on his right side.

"Follow me," Deacon's gruff voice demanded.

We didn't question Krampus. None of us wanted to be stuffed in his bag and beaten with switches. He led us beside the house.

Looking up at the windows, I could see the faces of the Yule Lads peeking over the window sills. They were spooked, too.

Deacon left huge prints in the snow as we followed him out past the barn to the edge of the forest.

"How far, Deac?" Troy asked.

"Not far," he replied.

He didn't lie. We stepped into the forest and within a few feet, I saw it. Tracks larger than Krampus feet. Also, a large worn spot in the snow like a huge beast had lain there. Empty beer bottles were littered around the crater.

"A beer drinking beast?" I asked.

"Yeti," Deacon said.

"There is no such thing," I said. I knew the beasts of the Otherworld. Some tales were just myths. The abominable snow monster was one of those myths.

"I do not lie," Deacon growled.

"Can we not piss off Krampus?" Levi suggested.

"Yep. My bad," I said.

Troy walked forward to inspect the footprints. He picked up one of the beer bottles and took a whiff. "Hmm, doesn't smell like anything I know."

The bottles were deep amber with no labels. "What, some kind of microbrew or something? Homebrew?" Levi asked.

"Possibly," Troy said.

"Anyone around here make beer?" I asked.

"I'm not sure, but we could ask Mike. I bet he would know. He makes all sorts of concoctions and has the supplies to do it," Troy said.

"He probably would know. Beer making and potion making are similar. It's all about alchemy," Troy replied. I would have to defer to his knowledge because it was something that I didn't know anything about.

"Perhaps he was just passing through," I suggested.

"Hope so," Levi replied as he put his foot in the center of one of the tracks. It stretched out almost a half foot on each side of his size thirteens.

"You know what they say about foot size," I suggested.

"Really?" he returned.

"Really." I smiled.

"I'm going to follow the tracks," Troy said.

"No way," I said. "You can't follow him alone." I shoved Levi toward him.

"Grace!" Levi protested.

"No, he won't be able to keep up," Troy said, handing Levi the lightning half of Driggs. The alpha wolf burst into a cloud of fur and nodded to us in assurance that he would be okay. Then, he dashed into the forest.

"Where did the other gun go?" I asked.

"Did you see his pouch?" Levi asked.

"No," I replied.

"He had a fur pouch made that he wears under his shirt. When he shifts, he puts the gun inside it. That way he has it if he has to shift back," Levi explained.

"That's rather ingenious," I said.

"Thank you," Levi replied.

"What? You didn't think of it," I scoffed.

"I did," he replied. "I've got all kinds of ideas."

"I bet you do." I brushed him off.

"Actually, I do have an idea for Dominick that I want to discuss with you," he said.

"Let's go home and discuss it," I said.

"Sure. Deacon, Troy will let us know what he finds. Try not to worry, and if anything happens, just give us a call. You know we have your back," Levi said.

Deacon nodded, as Levi grabbed my hand and opened the portal home.

CHAPTER SIX

"You are going to freak out," Aydan said, as he opened the door to greet us.

"Why?" I asked, suddenly alarmed. I could hear Bramble's voice barking out orders in the living room. We stepped inside to find at least 50 brownies standing in rows watching Bramble pace back and forth in front of them.

"Ten-hut! All hail the Queen!" he yelled.

"All hail the Queen!" they responded.

Levi snorted, and I elbowed him. "What the hell is this?" I asked.

"Your personal critter eradicating army," Bramble proclaimed.

Bramble had run off the squirrel from the attic, and I supposed he took our praise to heart after it happened.

"Bramble, I'm not sure we need a brownie army," I said.

"The way I see it, we are your only hope," Bramble insisted.

"The snow has driven the squirrels away," I said.

Bramble looked defeated.

"*Break his tiny heart, why don't you,*" Levi said. I tried to elbow him again, but he dodged it.

"Bramble, this is a great idea, and if the squirrels return, I know who to call," I said.

"Sure," he sniffed. Briar broke rank to grab his hand. She leered at me. There was no winning for me in this.

"Tomorrow, I will call the Handley's place and order them to make weapons for your troops," I said.

"You will?" Bramble asked.

"I promise," I said.

"Pirate cutlasses?" he asked.

"If that is what you want," I replied.

"It worked on the other squirrel," he reminded me.

"Of course, cutlasses it shall be," I said.

"You hear that! We are getting our own weapons!" Bramble yelled.

The troops lifted up a shrill cheer. I cringed at the noise.

"Alright, Bramble. Break it up," Levi insisted.

"Yes, of course, my King. Troops dismissed!" he yelled with a salute.

They saluted him back, then flew toward the front door. Aydan opened it swiftly as they flew out into the snowy night.

"Thank you, Bramble," I said.

"You are welcome, my Queen," he said with a bow. Briar took his hand, and they flew in the direction of Winnie's room with Thistle right behind them.

"You have your very own tiny army," Aydan said.

"Aydan, where have you and Callum been going?" I asked.

He looked stunned because I'd caught him off guard.

"We run in the woods mostly," he said.

"You fly?" I asked.

"Yes," he said. "Did we do something wrong?"

"No, but there is something lurking in the woods around Deacon's place," I said.

"Oh, okay. We can go check it out," he said.

"No!" Levi and I shouted.

He put his hands up in defense. "Okay. My bad. What is it?"

"We aren't sure yet. Just stay away from over there," Levi said.

"Stay out of the woods until we figure it out. Period."

"Mom," Aydan protested.

"No, Aydan, you heard me," I insisted.

"Yes, ma'am," he groaned.

"Where is Winnie?" I asked.

"She's up in her room," he replied with the same tone as before. "We picked her up on our way home."

"Little bird, I love you. I don't want anything to happen to you," I said.

"I know, Mom. I love you, too," he replied, but the tone didn't improve. He sighed, then climbed the stairs to his room.

"Was I too hard on him?" I asked Levi.

"Maybe a tad," he said, then kissed me on the temple. "But that's what mom's do. They love hard."

"I bet you were an angel child," I said, looking up at him. A devious grin appeared on his face which was not angelic.

"Mom loved me hard too," he said.

"Really?" I said, not believing him.

"I got into a few fights at school, which disappointed her. After she got sick, I cleaned up my act," he said. His blue eyes darkened as he spoke of his mother who had died of cancer.

"What were you fighting about? Girls?" I asked.

"No, nothing like that. You wish it was that, but it wasn't," he said, folding his fingers through mine. He tugged me over to the couch where we sat down right next to each other. "I was a pretty damn good baseball player, and I had the cocky attitude to go with it."

"So, that's where the smart remarks come from." I smiled, thinking about a smart-ass, teenaged Levi.

"Yeah, but when Mom got sick, I realized that I was being an ass. It was too late because she was already dying," he said.

"Did she get to see you like the sweet man that first came to me?" I asked.

"Something similar. By the time I got to you, I'd lost her and made a huge mistake with Lisette," he said. "Of course, I didn't think it was so huge then, but I know now how lucky I was that Jere-miah brought me to you. Otherwise, I'd probably be dead."

"Hush that dead talk. I can't handle it," I said.

"When I said that I wasn't leaving, I meant it," he said.

"If something happens to me, promise me you will take care of my children," I said.

His face winced in pain. "I don't know that I'd survive losing you."

"I thought the same thing about Dylan, but they were the ones that kept me going. Promise me, Levi," I insisted.

"Grace, you know I'd promise you the world if you wanted it. I promise," he said, pulling me closer to him and snuggling his face into my neck. "I promise."

AFTER GETTING Winnie ready for bed, Levi and I read her a story. She had to tell us about her day with Soraya. They wanted to have a sleepover, and I gave my permission. We slipped out of her room, and quietly shut the door. I'd barely heard the click, when Levi spun me around, then pressed me against the wall. His lips fell onto mine, hot and hungry. Something had given way in him. He wasn't holding back. My heart pounded in my chest with anticipation, as he pressed me harder against the wall. I tried holding back the moans as he kissed his way down my neck.

Using the wall as a prop, he lifted my legs to wrap around his waist but kept working my lips with his. The tingle became a throb-bing hum, as he walked us to the bedroom. He caught the bedroom door with his heel, slamming it closed.

"Now?" I muttered, as he lifted my sweater over my head.

"I can't wait any longer," he huffed. "You're driving me nuts."

I wasn't stopping him. I was more than ready. I'd learned the hard way that waiting for the things you want is just wasted time. Levi had claimed my heart as his from the moment he'd met me. He'd won it completely since Dylan's death. It was never about a victory for him, but making sure that our emotions were at the same place, at the same time.

The tattoo on his arm played the privacy tune enveloping us in a nice quiet bubble to ourselves. I tugged at his shirt, as he continued to kiss me. He released my lips long enough for me to pull it over his head. His hair mussed wildly. I dug my hands in it as he lowered his lips to my neck and shoulders. He took his time tasting every part of my skin.

"Levi," I sighed, as the tingle intensified.

"Hmm," he mumbled. The privacy bubble around us warbled, almost vibrating. I wasn't sure if it was his magic or our connection causing it. Then it warbled again.

"What is that?"

"Ignore it," he said, as the bubble fluctuated wildly.

"Something is wrong," I said.

"Fuck," he groaned, dropping the bubble. The warble changed to the ringing of his cellphone. "I didn't want to be completely out of touch if there is an emergency."

"Oh," I replied.

"Hello," he answered with a growl. "What? No, no. It's fine. I'll be there in a minute."

He hung up the phone and threw it across the room. Just before it hit the wall, I yelled, "Stop!" The phone hung in the air a couple of inches before it would have smashed into the wall.

"What is it?" I said, cupping his face with my hand.

"The squirrels are back in the storage at the Santiago place again. I've got to go help Troy," he groaned, looking down on the floor for his shirt.

"Levi," I whispered.

"What?" he huffed. Normally, I liked a good brood but now wasn't the time.

"I'll be here when you get back," I said. "Or I can go with you."

He hugged me tightly to his bare chest that was covered in sweat. He smelled like the bed I used to sleep in when he was in the Otherworld. Sandalwood and oranges. Dear goddess, Levi was all man and smelled like it.

"You stay with the kids. I won't be long," he said, planting a kiss on the top of my head. "I'm sorry."

"Levi, don't ever be sorry," I said. "Don't regret *any* moment we spend together."

"That's the fairy queen talking. All responsible and shit. I want Grace right now. Pitch a good fit for me," he huffed with a little laugh on the end.

"I don't think you could handle one of my fits," I replied. "Besides, you like me better this way."

"What I'd like is you to be naked on that bed over there and…" he stopped mid-thought and sighed again.

"Brood for me baby," I teased as he pulled his shirt back over his head.

"I'll be back soon. I love you, Grace," he said.

"Love you, too," I replied.

He rushed out of the door, grabbing the hovering phone along the way. With one final look at me before heading down the stairs, he made my heart ache and the fairy inside of me pitched the fit he wanted. At this rate, I was never going to get laid. Ever. Shady Grove didn't know how to let a woman or man have a moment's peace!

CHAPTER SEVEN

"How bad is it?" Nestor asked.

"Bad enough that he didn't come home," I said.

"Damn. Are you going out there?" he asked.

"Yeah, I stopped by to pick up some coffee for them. Then I'll go out there. Aydan and Callum are at home with Winnie. I've got to talk to Mr. Handley, too. I kinda promised Bramble's army that I would have him make weapons for them," I said, looking down into my mug of swirling glitter.

"Wait a minute. Bramble's army?" he asked.

"Bramble ran off the squirrel from our attic, so he has it in his head that he could form a brownie army. He demands that they all have pirate cutlasses," I explained.

"Pirate swords? Why?" he asked.

I shook my head. How did I explain this one? "Bramble, Briar, and Thistle have kinky roleplay sex. It was pirate day."

Nestor shook his head like someone had slapped him in the face. Just the smallest twitch. He held up his hand like he was going to say something, then swallowed his words.

"Exactly. Sometimes it's best *not* to know," I replied.

"How many of them are there?" he asked.

"I didn't count," I replied. "You don't have plastic olive skewers, do you? I saw some in a drink in Las Vegas. They could use those."

"Knowing Bramble, he won't be satisfied unless it's a real sword," Nestor teased.

"You are probably right," I said.

He poured a pot of his coffee into a large traveling container, then supplied me with foam cups and packets of sugar. "Hope that's enough," he said.

"It better be. I'm bringing my bard home with me," I said.

"I honestly never thought you would admit it," Nestor said.

"Admit what?"

"That you love him," Nestor said. "It took forever to do it with Dylan."

"And that is exactly why I admit it now. I wasted too much time when I could have been with him," I said.

"Grace, we don't know the future. It didn't matter how many times Jeremiah erased your memory, the two of you were going to be together," Nestor said.

"Eat your own words, Old Man, the next time you start feeling sorry for yourself about Mable. I've learned we live in a world of deception. Even with the sight we have as fairies, there are so many things that go unnoticed," I said.

He hung his head anyway. She had abused his trust and his heart, and one day I'd make her pay for it. I hadn't told him about the news we got from the frog in Vegas. Tennyson had yet to confirm if my mother, along with others, had escaped Brockton's wrath in the Otherworld. I didn't want to get his hopes up that his daughter was alive. If she was, then she knew where to find us and had chosen not to come here.

"Thank you, Grace," he mumbled.

"I love ya, Ness," I said.

WHEN I ARRIVED at the Santiago farm, the driveway looked like a police convention. Alongside Troy's cruiser were two others, plus a motorcycle which I assumed belonged to Dominick. Levi still wasn't riding his. He used the sword most of the time to get where he wanted to go or skipped. I pulled up in my truck as Troy and Dominick stepped out on the porch of the farmhouse.

"Howdy, boys! I've got Nestor's coffee," I said, climbing out of the truck.

"Thank the gods!" Troy exclaimed. Dominick rushed down the steps to take the items from me.

"He's down in the storage room," Nick said.

"How bad is it?" I asked.

"They tore through most of the exposed goods. Thankfully, she had canned and preserved a lot of it. The root vegetables were the biggest loss. Potatoes and carrots," he explained.

We walked up into the old farmhouse. I could hear the Santiago children playing upstairs. Mrs. Santiago stood in the kitchen slumped over the sink.

"Mrs. Santiago, could I offer you some coffee?" I asked.

"Grace! Welcome. No, thank you. Give it to the men working downstairs. This is such a horrid mess," she cried.

"Don't worry. Everything will be fine," I said, giving her a light pat on the shoulder. On the other side of the kitchen, a door stood open to stairs that went down. I could hear Levi's voice and followed it.

"Don't forget about those sacks in the back. All of them need to be checked," he ordered.

"Sure thing, Boss," I heard Lamar's voice. He had the Yule Lads here helping him.

Before I could get to the bottom step, he had skipped over to me, embracing me tightly.

"Morning," I said.

"I'm so sorry," he groaned.

I leaned back and placed my hand on his cheek. "It's all good. I'm here to work, so point me in the right direction. Oh! And Nestor sent coffee," I said.

"We are almost done. There had to be close to thirty of them down here when we stormed the place. They were huge. Like cats," Levi said.

"Big cats," Dominick added, while pouring Levi a cup of coffee. Levi took it from him with a nod. When he sipped, his shoulders relaxed and his excited tone quietened.

"We've got to get to the bottom of this. The only explanation is that someone sent them here. This isn't a case of natural migration," Troy said. I took his word for it since he knew animals better than I did.

"I don't see Brockton using the critters to get inside. Rhiannon might, on the other hand. It seems like it's right up her alley. The wench," I muttered.

"I agree," Levi said. "I'm not sure if she thinks she can force us out of the ward or if she's just trying to cause panic."

"I'm going to go with unrest and chaos, leading up to her moment to move in on us," Troy said. "Which brings me back to dear ol' Stephanie."

I sighed. I didn't know what to do with her other than I wanted her to pay for her crimes. "We need to have a meeting about what to do with her," I said.

"I'm good with just a snap, and she is gone," Troy said.

"Shh! I don't want Mrs. Santiago to hear you," I scolded.

"Crap," Troy muttered.

Lamar and Phillip appeared carrying two large sacks of potatoes. "These are still good, King Levi. Where do you want to put them?"

"Just set them down in this room. Anything that is ruined we will put outside. The back room should be empty before I get back," Levi instructed.

"You are leaving?" I asked.

"Yeah, I want you to come with me though," he said with a smile.

"Sounds good," I replied.

"Don't you care where we are going?" Levi asked.

"Nope," I replied. Troy grinned and nudged Levi who promptly swatted him off.

"I'll put the wards up when I get back," Levi said.

"We will wait for your return," Dominick replied. "We will have it all in here and keep the critters out while you are gone."

Levi nodded, then pulled out Excalibur from the sheath attached to his back. He used a spell to keep it masked until he put his hands on it. The blade sang as he twirled it in a circle. The magic of the swords was very powerful, but in Levi's hands, I wondered if Excalibur could be beaten. We stepped through into the snowy parking lot outside a rainbow glittered trailer.

"You are going to the vault?" I asked.

"Yes, I remember there being spells in Mable's book about summoning small beasts. I took it to mean, beasts. Like demons. But after seeing those giant squirrels, I knew it meant any animal. I think there is a counter-spell," he replied. "I memorized Talesin's book because the songs were natural to me. Mable's book is different."

"It's evil, and you don't have it in your heart to carry that around with you," I replied.

"If someone harmed you or the kids, I'm not so sure I wouldn't need someone to hold me back," he huffed. Perhaps my bard did have a dark bone or two.

"You are serious?" I asked.

"I don't think that there is anything in this world that could stop the rampage I would go on if I lost you."

"Levi, you can't let me taint your heart," I said.

"It's not tainted. It's completely and utterly surrendered to the fact that I cannot function without you," he said, lowering his head. "I'm whipped."

I cleared my throat, forcing myself not to take that tidbit and run with it. "You are your own strong man with or without me. If you are whipped, then you choose to be. But the next time you smart off or call me out on my shit, I'm going to remind you of how *not* whipped you are."

"You need that though," he said.

"Of course, and I wouldn't dare let anyone else get away with it."

"Makes me special." He wrapped his arms around me and

pulled me to him. Snow fell silently around us. The power I'd put into the storm was waning, but the snow would stay around for a while.

"You are my *special* bard," I laughed.

"You make it sound awful!" he protested.

"No! Not at all!"

"Come on. I've got to get the ward up before we lose the rest of the food stocks," he said but didn't let go. He rubbed his thumb over my cheek. Then kissed me.

Every time his lips touched mine, my hormones did flip-flops and that damn fairy lost her mind. He knew it too. The devil. In the midst of my enchantment, he stopped suddenly.

"Okay. That's enough of that," he said and tried to walk to the trailer but I held his hand. "What is it?"

"The first time I ever kissed you was in this parking lot," I said.

"Heh. A pretend kiss," he reminded me.

"It didn't feel like a pretend kiss," I replied.

"You hadn't decided what you wanted. Maybe you had, but you hadn't admitted it to yourself. In fact, the only reason you went with Amanda Capps that day was to try to save Dylan," Levi said.

"I'd do the same thing for you," I said.

"Back then, I would have called you a liar, but now, I know that you would," he admitted. "Now come on, it's freezing out here."

I shook my head. He wasn't cold. The conversation had moved to uncomfortable territory for him. It never occurred to me that he considered himself a second choice or leftovers after Dylan. I had to make sure he understood that he was so much more than that to me.

CHAPTER EIGHT

WHEN WE ENTERED THE DOMAIN OF MIKE, THE VAPE GUY, MY EYES teared up and a strong smell assaulted my nose.

"Hello, my Queen," Mike said with a nod.

"Hey, Mike. What's that smell?"

"Natural squirrel deterrent with a magical kick," he smiled. "In general, they don't like red pepper, so I've made a liquid that is hot peppers plus an added protection spell."

"That's why we were here. Levi was going to consult Mable's book about the invasion. It doesn't seem natural," I said.

"It's not. Normally the red pepper would keep them out, but I had to add the ward spell to it. Thankfully, they didn't get into my supplies," he said.

"I don't suppose you could make this stuff for everyone?" I asked.

"No. It would take too much time to produce that much. They would have eaten us out of house and home by then," he explained.

"We don't need it for everyone. We just need to protect our supplies," Levi said.

"I've got some left if you want to use it. I'd heard they got into the storeroom at the Santiago farm. How bad is it?" he asked.

"Pretty bad," Levi replied.

"Mike, have you ever come across a Yeti?" I asked.

"Several," he replied.

"Several!"

"Yep. There is at least one that lives nearby. He's a bigfoot though," he said.

"What's the difference?" I asked.

"Hair color mostly. Yetis are white. Bigfoots are brown," he explained.

"And Sasquatches?" Levi asked.

"Reddish-brown," he said. I think Levi meant it as a joke, but apparently, there were several different species of the creature.

"Beer drinkers?" I asked.

"Sometimes. Why?"

"We found tracks and some empty beer bottles in the woods near Deacon Giles' farm," I told him.

"The one I know of doesn't drink. He's Amish," he said.

"The Amish drink," Levi said.

"This one doesn't. He's New World Amish. Very strict. They even practice bundling," he said.

"What the fuck is that?" Levi asked.

"Not fucking," I replied. "A betrothed couple can sleep in the same bed if they are wrapped tightly."

Levi looked at me, then a grin spread across his face. "Grace, how do you know that?"

I shrugged, "It's not my fault that he wasn't bundled well enough."

Mike slapped the countertop with a hearty laugh. "Seducing the Amish!"

"I never said I was a good person," I replied.

"No more Amish," Levi said with a laugh.

"No, I'm all about celibacy now. Might as well become a nun."

Levi grunted. Mike knew better than to comment on that one.

"Want to go check the book?" I asked.

Levi nodded, and Mike opened the secret door to our vault of Otherworld treasures.

Descending the steps, the crystals in the wall responded to my presence, lighting our way to the portal door. Levi stepped through first, and I followed quickly behind. Torches in the room blazed the moment we appeared on the inside.

"Where did those come from?" I asked.

"I thought it was a cool touch," he grinned.

"How much time do you spend down here?" I asked.

"Not as much as I used to. I'd much rather be helping the town and be with you," he said.

"Aw, aren't you just the sweetest," I said, bunching my lips up at him. He cut his eyes to me then huffed.

"I can't help it. You just bring it out of me," he replied, dripping sarcasm.

"Bravo! I wondered if you could do bitter sarcasm. That was perfect," I complimented him.

"I learned from the best," he snipped.

I put my hands over my heart and gasped. "Oh, you hurt me, Levi." I laughed.

"Keep it up, and I'll show you right here how sweet I can be," I said.

"Naughty, naughty," I laughed.

"Here is just as good as anywhere," he huffed.

"Sure," I replied.

He took Mable's book off the shelf then plopped down in the recliner. "Wanna sit?" he asked, patting his lap.

Levi Rearden was asking for trouble that he wasn't prepared to handle. Stalking over to him, he watched me sway like a fool, before straddling his lap in the old recliner. Mable's book dropped to the floor and his hands grasped my waist. I rocked back and forth on his lap, and he purred like a kitten.

"No, I don't want to sit," I said, leaning over his mouth. His hands snaked up my back under my shirt. Calloused and rough. Pushing downward on my spine, he forced my mouth to his glorious lips. Levi flourished in intimate conditions. It was mesmerizing. I attributed it to his love talker side. He knew exactly where to touch me, when to push it, and when to hold back.

"I lose all focus when you are like this," he said, kissing my neck.

"I'm like this all the time," I replied.

"I know. I can't damn focus," he growled, digging his fingers into my back. I felt him beneath me. Aroused and ready.

I jerked my shirt over my head, and he planted his face between my breasts.

"Grace! Levi! Grace! Levi! Help us!" Shouts came from above.

"Mother fuck!" Levi growled, standing up, but holding me in place so I could put my feet on the ground. "Put your shirt on!"

I laughed. "Yes, Sir!"

He ran out of the portal back into Mike's shop. I picked up Mable's book and placed it back on the shelf, and reluctantly put on my shirt.

"Calm down!" Levi shouted at Cletus and Tater.

They were talking over each other non-stop. I wasn't sure which one said what.

"It was enormous!"

"Ginormous!"

"And it had fangs like a snake, but bigger like a..."

"Sabertooth tiger."

"Yeah, that thing. He wore a backpack made of steel and..."

"He roared like a lion..."

"And he beat his chest like a gorilla. Like that one in Tarzan. The mean one."

"And he threw bottles at us..."

"He was white all over," Cletus finished up the description.

"What was it?" I asked.

"A giant wild man," Tater said. "My pawpaw seen one out in these parts back when he was alive. He said that he would take dogs and cattle and eat them."

"Bigfoot," Levi said.

"I seen 'em too! Tater ain't lyin'," Cletus added.

"No, we don't think you are lying," I replied.

"You better hide that weiner dog of yours," Tater suggested.

"I'll advise Rufus to stay inside," I promised.

"Focus. Where did you see him?" Levi asked. His patience had grown thin.

"*Levi,*" I scolded.

"*I'm so wound up that I can't control it,*" he huffed. Last year, he would have stomped out of the room and slammed a door, but now, he took a deep breath then focused on Cletus and Tater.

"We was out near Dylan's old place," Tater said.

"No, we were in the woods near the hedge maze," Cletus replied.

"No, we were near the Riggs farm," Tater countered.

"I think I'd remember where we were since we were on our own property!" Cletus replied.

"Oh, maybe we were," Tater relented.

"You own the property with the hedge maze?" Levi asked.

"Yep. My uncle was a crazy old bastard, and he built that maze. The rumor is that he had a mess of Spanish gold and hid it out there somewhere, but we've looked everwher' for it," Cletus said.

"We dug holes from there to the county line and didn't find a damn thing," Tater said.

"Guys, focus. The bigfoot. Where did you see him?" I asked.

"Cletus is right. It was out near the maze," Tater conceded.

"I'll call Tennyson," Levi said.

"No, you and I should go," I said.

"Alright. What about the spell book?" Levi asked.

"We need to outsource some of these king/mayor duties," I replied.

"To the queen," he added.

"No, not to me. To our knights. We've got a brand new one," I said.

"Dominick doesn't know magic," Levi said.

"No, but Astor does," I said.

"He does?"

"He's not all ginger brute. When he swore his oath to me, he formed a solid circle of protection around us. I imagine being the only son of Morgana, he knows quite a few things," I said.

Levi sighed, "I feel like it's my responsibility."

"It is, but it doesn't mean your hands have to do it. It just means that you have to make sure it gets done," I said.

"I'll call Astor," he relented.

"Brilliant idea. I wish I had thought of it," I said with a wink.

He sneered at me and fished out his phone.

"Can we go with y'all? I wanna get a picture of it," Cletus asked.

"No, I think it's best you boys go home. That bigfoot might not be a friendly creature," I said. "I'd hate it if something happened to you."

"Alright, but if he's nice, then can we go get a picture?" Cletus persisted.

"Maybe," I replied.

"Yes!" Cletus said and bumped fists with Tater.

"I said, maybe!"

"Good enough for me," Cletus laughed as they left me alone with Levi and Mike.

"Those two are the best foragers I've ever had," Mike said.

"Huh?"

"I pay them to hunt up natural ingredients that I need for the liquid spells," Mike explained. "They know this area better than anyone. I think that might be an advantage to you."

"I worry about them being here with all the trouble that goes on," I said.

"Don't worry about them. I keep an eye out for them, plus you can't underestimate a couple of rednecks who know how to rough-neck," he said with a grin.

"I suppose not, but I did see them try to attach a grill to the side of a trailer once," I said thinking back.

"Ha! They told me about that. The execution wasn't perfect, but it was a mighty fine idea," Mike said. "Here. Take what's left of the liquid and use it at the Santiago farm. I'll see about whipping some more up."

"Thanks," I said.

Cletus and Tater did have a knack for primitive engineering. I supposed it was normal to have a trial and error phase before they perfected their creations. I remembered the giant boat that they tried to make out of bottles which ended up being destroyed, but the little rafts they made from them were perfect. Astor could attest to the effectiveness of their potato gun. It took a month for that welt to go away even with fairy healing. Maybe Cletus and Tater had their uses, but I still worried about their lives. Even though they weren't like the rest of us, they were my subjects, and I would protect them to the best of my ability.

CHAPTER NINE

LOOKING AROUND THE HEDGE MAZE, I SHOOK MY HEAD. "YOU'VE got to be kidding me."

"They weren't lying about digging everything up," Levi said.

The maze itself was intact, but around the clearing and into the woods surrounding the maze, mounds of earth littered the landscape where Cletus and Tater had been looking for Spanish gold.

"Maybe the bigfoot wants the gold too," Levi suggested.

I laughed. "Maybe that's it. I just want to see him."

"Never seen one?" he asked.

"Nope. You?"

"Other than Astor after a shower, which was an accident. That man is hairy," Levi said, wrinkling his nose.

"He probably doesn't kiss as good as Dylan either," I said.

Levi nudged me with his elbow. "You haven't brought that up in a while," he said.

"Meh. I like to sprinkle it in when it's most effective," I explained.

"I miss him," Levi admitted. We didn't talk about Dylan much. He was sparing my feelings on it, but I wanted to talk about him. He wasn't important only to me. He touched all of our lives. I kissed him on the cheek in acceptance of his admission to let him know it was okay to feel that way. I was to the point where I could talk about it, and remember our time happily.

"So, Sasquatch," I said.

"Yeah," he smiled. He looked from me to the woods around the maze. He'd switched to fairy sight. "There is something to the west. Don't take any chances with this thing."

His eyes centered back to me, and I waved my two ice swords at him. He reached behind his back and pulled out Excalibur. Together we headed toward the west and the glow of something cold and winter.

A quick strum of his tattoo, and our footsteps silenced as we marched through the snow. The glow increased the deeper we went into the woods. A path led to a thicket of dense pines. Empty bottles littered the ground from us to as far as we could see. If the creature was drinking all of these, I was going to suggest an Abominable Alcoholics Anonymous. Levi picked up one of the bottles, then took a whiff.

"Definitely beer, but with a sweeter smell," he said.

"Maybe there is a drip left in the bottom and you can taste it," I said lifting an eyebrow.

"Grace, that's gross," he said, tossing the bottle back down. "I'll get Cletus and Tater to pick up all these bottles. They told me the other day they were collecting glass."

"Glass?"

"I didn't ask," he said.

Reaching out with my senses, I could hear the rustling of the underbrush just ahead of us. I grabbed Levi's arm, and he froze in place.

"*What?*"

"*I hear something,*" I told him.

He pulled power from an oak tree to our right. I felt the surge of nature rush toward him. With every day, he was becoming more and more powerful. I wasn't sure how it was possible, but I think it had to do with his pure heart. The power of nature was drawn to him. The same way that it was with my darkness.

He picked up the pace unafraid of whatever awaited us. I followed along with him. The noise ahead of us ceased. We rushed into a small clearing hoping to catch a glimpse of the fabled creature, but there was nothing. Not even footprints. Snow fell lightly around us, but besides that, nothing moved and the woods fell silent.

"Weird," Levi said.

"If he is a magical being, then he can probably skip or do something like it. Perhaps he goes invisible," I said.

"No, looking through my sight I don't even see the residue of a spell or magic," Levi said.

"Might be a different kind of magic than what we are used to seeing," I said.

"Perhaps," Levi said.

I slipped my hand into his, and he squeezed it. I closed my eyes and thought about the parking lot at the Foodmart, and we skipped back to town.

～

LEVI WENT with me to visit Sylvester Handley. We ordered two dozen tiny cutlasses for the brownie army. If they needed more, it would have to wait. Sly and his son were working overtime making weapons for the war with Brockton. I walked through the storage of what they already had prepared. It was mostly swords and daggers.

"I'm waiting on some new material to come in to make armor. I'm going to try using some aluminum. It's lightweight, and Mike, the vape guy, tells me he has a magical hardener that will make it tougher with no added weight," Sly explained. He stood with us wearing a denim apron over heavy duck pants with a button up shirt. His grey hair reached down his temples with Elvis style sideburns.

"We will run some tests on it before we mass produce it," Levi added.

"When do you expect the material?" I asked.

"In a couple of days. It's hard to get aluminum around here

because so many automotive manufacturers are using it on their vehicles," he said.

"But Tennyson has sources," I surmised.

"He does," Levi confirmed.

I took a deep breath looking at the weapons which represented the lives that will be in danger and possibly lost. The time was soon approaching that I would need to ask the town personally for their help, and lay out the consequences for it. It had to be done, and we needed all the help we could get, but at the same time, I loved these people. They, as a whole, brought me out of the shell I'd built for myself. They were my friends and family, even the ones I didn't particularly like. I swore to do right by them.

Levi's arms enveloped me as his breath brushed across my ear. "Don't let it daunt your resolve."

"So many lives in our hands," I said.

"We will give them the choice," he said.

"Even so, most of them came here to live quietly in their banishment. When Jeremiah brought me here, it jeopardized all of them," I said.

"When Jeremiah picked me up, it was a long drive through Mississippi to Shady Grove, and during that time, he talked a lot. I was too caught up in my own problems to really pay attention to him, but one thing I do remember is that he said that you would change my life. He said that you were stubborn, beautiful, dangerous, and powerful, but beneath the surface, you had more heart than any fairy he had ever known. I know your opinion of him isn't high, and we still don't know exactly whose side he was on, but I think he truly admired you. Those things stuck with me, and despite my brooding, you reached through and touched me. I've loved you ever since. I believe he brought us both here for this. For what was coming. He always seemed to know the future, and I didn't understand even though he denied it. Grace, we were meant to do this," he said.

"And Dylan?"

"Jeremiah was giving you options," Levi said. "Remy is here, too. Who knows who else he would have brought here to compliment you? To support you through this. You've allowed me to have a bigger role, but I will never be delusional to think this isn't about you."

I smiled at that idea. My own harem. I could never do it. My heart had found the intimate connection to one person to be the best for me. Levi had my heart now. Earned it. More than earned it. And I'd have to thank Jeremiah one day for that. Dylan had a subtle way to reinforce me and kept me in line. Levi was much more direct. And even though I hadn't slept with Levi, I knew, Dylan was direct in the bedroom where he wasn't everywhere else. I had the feeling Levi was subtle and would feed off my needs. Both of them complimented me in different ways.

I turned around so I could look at him, face to face. Putting my palms on his cheeks, I leaned in close to kiss him. "It's not about me. It's about us," I said, just before my lips brushed across his. He let out a heavy sigh, then returned the kiss.

CHAPTER TEN

WHEN I RETURNED HOME, WINNIE AND MARK HAD GONE OUT INTO the woods toward the circle to play. Marshall, the head of my centaur guards, informed me that two of his best men had gone with them along with the brownies.

Aydan and Callum were inside making sandwiches. The boys ate constantly. I didn't think either of them was growing particularly fast, but they consumed calories like food was scarce. And I supposed, to an extent, it was, since the food storage got hit by the squirrels.

Levi had returned to the vault to get Mable's book and find the solution he needed to protect the food storage. Astor had called and was having issues setting up a ward there, and Levi had promised to go back out to the farm with Mike's bottle of magical red pepper liquid. It looked like it would be another long night alone.

I made a couple of sandwiches for Winnie and Mark and decided to go out to the circle myself. Returning there reminded me of my father. The power held within the stone that connected to the Tree of Life protected that circle. Outside of our home and the vault, Winnie and Mark were in the safest place in Shady Grove.

Trekking through the woods in the snow, I listened for unusual movements or anything that might signal the beer-drinking bigfoot was nearby. I heard nothing.

As I got closer to the circle, I could hear Winnie and Mark. The pair had their ups and downs, but for the most part, Mark stayed loyal to Winnie while she worked out her issues. Two centaurs stood outside the stone circle watching for danger. I greeted them with a smile then passed through the outer rim of stones. A small fire blazed near the center stone. It wasn't big enough to be harmful. Winnie and Mark sat on the stone near the little fire.

"Momma!" she called out as I drew near.

"Hi! I brought sandwiches," I said, holding up the paper bag that I had packed them in.

"Thanks! I'm starved," Mark said.

I stepped into the circle, and the stones greeted me by flaring up with blue Winter power.

"That's so cool," Winnie said.

"It's my circle, so it recognizes me," I said.

"Are the stones alive?" Winnie asked.

"No, not alive. But they hold power. The same kind of power that I keep inside of me," I explained.

"Winnie has that power, too," Mark added.

"Yes, she does," I confirmed. Winnie shook her head. "She's still trying to figure it out though."

"What prompted the hike into the woods?" I asked them.

"Mark wanted to talk to me about having brothers," Winnie said while chomping on a ham sandwich. I sat down with them on the triquetra stone. It was the only spot not covered in snow.

"My mom is pregnant," Mark muttered.

"Does that upset you?" I asked.

"Kind of. I didn't think she would have any more kids. Dad didn't want any," he said.

"Sometimes people want things, and they don't even realize it. I bet when your siblings arrive, your Dad will be excited to see them," I said.

"He will, for sure. Then he will have his own kids," Mark said, staring at his sandwich.

"Mark, Troy Maynard loves you like his own child. Just like I love Winnie. To me, there is no difference between her and Aydan. Hell, you can add Callum to that too."

"Winnie said you don't treat her any differently," Mark admitted.

"I don't. If I do, it's not on purpose," I said.

"She still makes me clean my room and eat my vegetables," Winnie laughed.

"I still read her bedtime stories and cuddle on the couch watching movies," I added.

Mark sighed, and Winnie reached over to pat him on the hand. "You are being a silly boy, Mark Maynard. Your daddy loves you, just like mine loved me. Don't you remember him coming to save us from Miss Robin? He'd give his life for you," Winnie said.

I could not have formed the argument any better myself. Tears welled up in the sides of Mark's eyes. "Yes, he would."

"See. You're being silly," Winnie reinforced. When I gave her the "mom look," she backed off the harsh statement. She was too much like me. Comforting him, but teasing him at the same time. "You are lucky to have a dad like that."

"I agree," I said.

Mark nodded, then joined us in eating sandwiches.

"Where are Bramble and Briar?" I asked.

"They said they had important army business," Winnie said.

I rolled my eyes. This brownie army was getting out of hand. Their directive was to keep an eye on Winnie, not traipse around in the woods looking for squirrels. It was time to have a talk with the brownies about their purpose in our life. Brownies were known to be extremely loyal but easily distracted. Plus, I needed to have a talk with Thistle. She wasn't part of our original agreement. I needed to be sure she was on the same page as the other two if she was going to be in my house on a regular basis.

"You guys ready to go home?" I asked.

"I am," Winnie declared. She jumped up, brushing crumbs off her sweater and jeans.

"I don't want to go home," Mark muttered.

"I don't mind if you stay with us, but at some point, Mark, you will need to go home and be the big brother that your siblings will need. They will count on you to protect them like you protect Winnie. They will adore you for it."

"I guess," he shrugged.

"Come on. Let's go call your parents," I said.

We walked back to the house in silence. Winnie skipped, and Mark trudged along behind me, kicking snow. The centaur guards followed further behind, but close enough to intervene if we needed help.

WHEN LEVI CAME HOME, it was still dark outside, but early in the morning. I had fallen asleep on the couch. Mark and Winnie decided to camp out in the living room. He sat on the edge of the couch as I offered a groggy smile.

"Hi," he whispered.

"Hi, welcome home," I replied.

"I'm going to get a shower," he said.

"You look exhausted," I replied.

"Too much magic," he muttered.

I knew that feeling. After throwing it around for a while, magic had a way of exhausting you like a long workout.

"Get a shower, then sleep," I suggested.

He kissed me on the forehead. "Yes, ma'am."

I listened as the shower turned on upstairs in his bathroom. Before long, the water shut off, and his footsteps padded quietly above me. His presence suddenly moved closer. I opened my eyes to find him crawling onto the couch with me. I shuffled my body so that I'd be lying partially on top of him. His chest moved up and down slowly. The heavy breaths of a deep sleep filled the room. Snuggling up next to him, my heart warmed feeling the tingle between us. It was a feeling of safety and love. It felt like home.

CHAPTER ELEVEN

THE NEXT MORNING, I PREPARED A FULL BREAKFAST FOR EVERYONE IN the house. Callum and Aydan came home very late after Levi got home. They got the evil mom eye from me. Aydan dropped his head in penance, but it wasn't enough.

The smell of bacon filled the house as I scrambled eggs and baked biscuits. Winnie and Mark were in charge of setting the table. They chatted about the new cartoon on the television. Levi helped me with breakfast by taking drink orders and rousing the boys. Aydan and Callum sauntered in with wild hair and groggy faces.

Sitting down for a meal with my family always recharged my well-being. I loved listening to the chatter. Aydan progressively awoke more as he ate and teased Winnie about her hair and having a boy over. Winnie returned the favor by scolding him for staying out too late. He cut his eyes to me, and then back to Winnie. He had a better chance of winning with her than with me.

"*This is what it is all about,*" Levi said.

"*Yes, it is,*" I replied with a smile.

After we finished, Aydan and Callum were voluntold to clear the table and do the dishes. Voluntold was when you were told to volunteer. They didn't grumble, because they knew they were on the hot seat.

"Mom and Dad are here," Mark muttered as a car pulled up outside.

"Winnie, go open the door for them," I instructed as I finished returning all the condiments from breakfast to the fridge and pantry.

"Come on in," I heard Winnie say.

"Good morning, Winnie," Amanda said cheerfully. She didn't sound like herself. Amanda had always been pretty severe. I peeked around the corner to get a look at her. Her belly protruded from her small frame.

"Oh, my goddess!" I exclaimed.

"It happened quickly," she said.

"Is that normal?" I asked.

"We've known for a while. I've just hidden it," she admitted.

"Oh, I see. What does the doc say?" I asked.

"Tabitha says everything is fine. Very normal," she said.

"Congratulations!" I exclaimed finally.

"Thank you," she replied with a blush. Troy stood behind her. He looked like a skunk crawled up his butt and died.

"You look beautiful."

"Yes, you do," Levi agreed. "Doesn't she, Troy?"

"*Oh, you stepped in it,*" I teased.

"*He needs to get over himself. It's not like she did it on her own,*" Levi pointed out.

"She is gorgeous," Troy answered, but the facial expression didn't change.

Mark cowered next to Winnie, and I realized what had pissed off Troy.

"Alright! Everyone upstairs. Aydan, Callum, Winnie. Now!" I demanded.

The dishes clattered in the kitchen as the boys rushed at my command. No magic needed. Just mom voice. Winnie kissed Mark on the cheek which caused him to blush deeply. I winked at her as she passed me to run up the stairs.

Mark stood alone in the center of the living room. He lifted his chin ready for whatever his father had to say.

"Thank you, Grace, but this is a family matter and we will talk about it at home," Troy said.

"Well, that's fine, but we are going to talk about it here, too," I replied.

"I agree," Amanda said. She walked over and took a seat on the couch. I was pretty sure Levi would take our side, so Troy didn't have a row to hoe with us.

"Would y'all like some coffee?" Levi asked. Everyone shook their head.

Troy reluctantly sat down next to Amanda who opened her arms for Mark. The poor little wolf shook his head. "Mark, come talk to me," Amanda pleaded.

"You should have come home last night," Troy said.

"I wanted to stay with Winnie," Mark murmured.

"Why?" Troy asked.

"Because she invited me to stay," he said, pointing at me.

"I thought he needed a night away from home. I apologize to you both, if I overstepped my boundaries, but he was upset. Just as he protects Winnie, she comforts him," I explained.

"Why are you upset?" Amanda asked.

"I don't want siblings," he huffed. "Dad doesn't even want them."

"Hold up there now, Partner," Troy said. "It wasn't what I planned for us, but I'm excited to have new members of the family. You will be a great big brother."

Mark hung his head, staring at his shuffling feet. "Nothing could make us love you less," Amanda coaxed.

When I was younger, my father sat me on his lap and told me that I had lots of brothers, but that he loved me more than any of them. It was a wrong thing for him to do. Now that I had my own children, I knew that my heart loved each of them fully. Perhaps Father thought it would encourage me to accept my role as his heir. It didn't matter. I saw the look in Finley's eyes when he overheard our conversation. No child should feel like they are less than another.

"Mark, come here, Son," Troy requested.

Mark walked over to him slowly, and Troy scooped him up as soon as he came in range. Mark whimpered into Troy's shoulder as he hugged the boy tightly.

"I love you, Dad," Mark said.

"I love you, too. But listen to me, I was wrong to be upset about your mom having more kids. They will be a great part of our family, and I will be proud of all of you. I will love you just as much as I love them."

Levi's arm wrapped around my waist, and I leaned into him.

"You will have a lot of responsibility to help show them our ways," Amanda said. "They will be the children of the Alpha."

"What does that make me?" Mark asked.

"My first son," Troy said with pride. "You will always be my first son."

Amanda wiped the tears from Mark's cheeks and kissed Troy gently. "Thank you," she whispered.

"I've been a little bit stupid," Troy said.

"Scared is more like it," Amanda said.

Levi tugged, and I followed him into the hallway just beyond the kitchen. "I thought we'd give them a little privacy."

"Yeah. I knew he would come around," I said.

"Did you?"

"Yep," I replied. He wanted to ask me something. I felt it on the tip of his tongue as our minds were so connected. He hesitated. "Go ahead. Ask."

He bit his bottom lip and shook his head. For a moment, it reminded me of that young unsure man who stepped into my trailer last year.

"Levi," I coaxed. "It's okay."

"Do you think you will have any more?"

"I don't know. I never thought I'd have one, much less the three that are here now. It's something we can discuss once this war is over. I understand Troy's hesitation. The last thing I want to do is bring a child into this mess," I said. "No more than I already have. Do you want to be a father?"

"I hadn't really thought about it until just now. I know I'm just Uncle Levi to your kids, but I love them like they are mine," he said.

"I could fuck you right here for saying that," I said, laughing.

"Grace! Damn," he sighed.

He captured my wrists in his hands and pushed me against the wall with his body. Holy hell! He knew how to shock me with his advances. Just a moment ago, he was unsure as a kitten in a new litter box, but now he was Mister Sexual Aggression. Instead of kissing my lips, he kissed my cheek, my ear, and my neck. I sighed with pleasure. Each peck sent a thrilling tingle through my body like little taser jolts.

"Grace, we are going to head home," Troy called out to us. Levi released me immediately, and I tried to regain my senses as I stepped back into the living room.

"Oh, okay. He is welcome to stay anytime," I said. Troy grinned at me.

"He needs to stay home and get used to his responsibilities with the pack. I might have been too hard on him, but he's got to learn," Troy said.

"Maybe he's got a gypsy soul," I suggested.

"His gypsy butt has a pack," Troy said. There was humor in his voice, but I could tell he was frustrated. "He will learn. He's still young."

"He's a good boy," I said.

"Yeah. He is," Troy said. "Catch you later, Levi."

"Later," Levi said as Troy walked out the door. "Now, where were we?"

Levi's hands rested at my waist, pulling me back towards him.

A light tapping at the back door interrupted us before we could even get started.

"I swear. Someone behind that door is going to die," Levi grumbled.

He stomped to the back door, throwing it open.

"Hello, my King," Bramble said from the porch. Levi looked

down, and I moved forward to see the brownie. He leaned on Briar, and they swayed back and forth. They almost toppled forward when Bramble tried to bow, but Briar kept them upright.

"What the hell?" I muttered.

"We found this nice guy with beer," Bramble said with a hiccup.

"Really good beer," Briar added.

"Are you drunk?" I asked.

"I believe we are," Bramble said. "What say you, my Dear?"

"Totally drunk," she replied.

"Good grief," Levi muttered. "Was it the Yeti?"

"Yes! At first, he was mad, because I called him abomin... adomin...amodim…"

"Abominable," I suggested.

Bramble snapped his finger and pointed at me. "That's it, but he forgave us. Then, he shared his beer."

"It was so good and sweet. Like honey. Like my little, honey, woney," Briar said while poking Bramble in the side.

"Where is Thistle?" I asked.

"She left. She doesn't like beer. She's a party pooper," Briar said.

"Sounds like she was the smart one," Levi muttered.

"Get inside before you pass out," I commanded.

"I'm pretty sure that I can't walk another step," Bramble said, then promptly fell face forward to the floor with a tiny thud. Briar gasped and fell to her knees next to him.

"Oh! My love! Don't die now!" Briar pleaded.

"He's not dead," Levi said, reaching down to pick up Bramble. Briar hitched a ride on his hand too. "I'll take them up to Winnie's room to the dollhouse."

"Good idea. Tell the boys they can finish the dishes. When Bramble and Briar sober up, maybe they can lead us to the yeti," I said.

"He's not hurting anything. He hasn't attacked anyone. Maybe we should just focus on the squirrels," Levi suggested.

"Maybe," I replied, as he walked up the stairs with the two little brownies in his hand.

Aydan and Callum returned to their kitchen duties without any prompting. Levi instructed Winnie to take care of the brownies and let us know when they woke up. Any details they had about our visitor would be helpful in knowing his intentions within the protection of our town. In the meantime, I'd gotten at least ten calls about squirrel incidents. The snow had not deterred the little bastards. I could hear at least one scratching in my attic again.

However, when Levi called Mrs. Santiago, she confirmed that the food storage had been kept safe by Mike's magical red pepper liquid. That was at least one victory. Michael Handley called to tell us that the brownies' weapons were done.

Levi decided to make the rounds to the houses where people were complaining about the squirrels, and I made my way into town to get the tiny weapons. Aydan and Callum promised to stay home with Winnie. Rufus sat on his tush and didn't do anything. Such a productive member of the family.

Sylvester Handley presented me with 50 tiny cutlasses. He decided to make a few extra, because he said brownies had a way of multiplying. I thanked him, and he requested that one of the brownie army visit his attic. He was having the same trouble as the rest of us.

"If only squirrels could talk," I said.

"There are beings that can talk to animals, but as far as I know, there isn't anyone in Shady Grove who can," Sly said.

"I've heard that there were, but I've never seen it myself," I replied.

"Perhaps ask the gypsies. They have strange ways," he suggested.

"I might do that. I've been meaning to visit Wendy," I agreed.

"Have a good day," he said as he returned to making the bigger weapons for our war for Winter.

I drove my big truck out to the gypsy RV camp. I passed the field where Dylan died, and I couldn't force myself to look that way. When I pulled up to the RVs, the camp was uncharacteristically quiet. I assumed that had to do with the snow.

When I approached Wendy's RV, I heard chanting inside. Three voices in unison speaking in a language that I didn't recognize.

Switching to my sight, I saw strands of magical power leaking out of the RV in different directions. I waited, not wanting to interfere with the spell. Whether it was good or bad, you didn't want to stop one of those things in the middle. Half-hitched spells were trouble.

The chanting died down, and Wendy opened the door to greet me.

"Come in out of the cold!" she insisted, even though the cold didn't bother me.

I stepped inside to find an altar on the table in the RV. Kady and Riley sat on their knees on the floor staring at it. Incense burned in a small wooden bowl giving off a spiraling stream of white smoke. A purple cloth in the center featured a pentacle. Two candles burned: one black and one white.

"I'm sorry that I interrupted," I whispered.

"It's fine. We were just working on some blessings for the new year," Wendy explained. "We are also trying to speak to the horned god to get guidance on the bushy-tailed invaders."

"I was going to ask you about that," I admitted. "We've pretty much tried everything, and they are still around. Someone suggested finding someone who could speak to animals. I don't know of anyone in Shady Grove with that ability."

"Our people have been known to converse with creatures great and small, but I admit that no one in our gathering has that ability."

The door to the RV rattled, and Fordele, Wendy's husband, walked in.

"Howdy, Grace," he said with a smile.

"Hi, Ford," I replied. It surprised me to see him there. The last I'd heard, he had moved out of Wendy's RV.

"What's going on in here?" he asked.

"Just a protection meditation and trying to contact the horned god," Wendy explained.

"Well, the Jeffries' place on the back side of the park got hit by the squirrels. They ate all their provisions. What are y'all doing about this, Grace? Isn't that your department?"

"Ford, Grace can't control animals," Wendy scolded.

"She is the *Queen*," Ford sneered.

"You can leave," Wendy said.

"I'd rather the rest of you get out of my RV."

"Ford, what has gotten into you?" I asked.

"He's ready to leave, but the rest of us want to stay," Wendy said.

"You are my wife!" he yelled at her.

"That is about enough of that," I interjected. "You are acting like one of those squirrels crawled up your butt."

"He'd probably like that," Riley snipped from behind me.

"You! This is all your fault." Ford pointed at her, and I stood between them. "You are the one that started all of this witchy stuff."

"I was a witch long before Riley came along," Wendy pointed out.

"You weren't a practicing one," Ford said.

"Maybe I was and you just didn't realize it," she taunted.

"What?"

"I could have made you do whatever I wanted," she continued. I had to laugh at her playing him. He deserved it after his outburst. "Ford, you need to calm down. Go back in the back, and I'll come to you soon."

"If he talked like that to me, he could keep his gravy to himself," I laughed.

"It's been a long time since I've heard it called gravy," Riley mused.

"Me too," Kady added.

"Okay. That's more uncomfortable than I want to be right now," I said. "Keep me informed if you make any progress."

"Come on, Grace. Now that you've had him. Tell us what you think," Riley pushed.

"I don't share that kind of information with anyone," I replied.

"You could tell us. We already know what he's like in bed," Kady added.

"Right. So, I'll be catching all of you later." I made a bee-line to the door, when Riley took her last punch.

"You haven't even slept with him, and you were mad at us for toying with his heart. You could destroy him," Riley scolded.

"That's enough," I said, then stepped outside. I refused to participate in that kind of conversation. There was a time when I would have jumped down her throat, and she would have deserved it. However, I wasn't that person anymore.

I sat down in the truck and put my head on the steering wheel. Was I leading him on? Surely, we could find time to do it if we really wanted. Why was I holding back? Why was I all of the sudden questioning myself because Riley decided to be Riley? I sighed, then lifted my head to start the truck.

"Hi," Levi said next to me.

"Mother fuck!" I wasn't sure how he managed to arrive without tipping me off, but he had.

"Sorry," he laughed. "What's wrong?"

"You can feel that?"

"Yes."

"Riley and Kady were prying into our private business."

"Really?"

"Wanted to know what I thought of you."

"Thought of me?" he questioned.

"Don't play dumb," I huffed.

"Grace, look at me."

Slowly I turned my head to him. I saw humor dancing in his eyes. His smile was infectious, and I had to resist returning it.

"What?"

"We have forever, Grace."

"You think that, but perhaps we don't," I said.

"We do," he insisted. "Now, let's go to the diner. I'm starved."

"The diner is closed because of the snow," I reminded him.

"Then drive me home and feed me, Woman," he said.

Turning the key in the ignition, I leered at him as the truck fired up. He slid across the seat right next to me. I turned my face away from him, but he put one hand on my right cheek forcing me to look at him.

His blue eyes were bright and playful as he leaned in for a kiss, but just before his lips touched mine, he said, "Home."

The world around us blurred, then reformed. He had ported us and the truck back to the house.

"Good grief, Levi," I said.

"I know," he replied. "I can do a lot of things."

"I always knew you could, but porting a whole four door pick-up. That's really impressive," I said.

"We are going to win this fight," he said.

"Yes, we are," I replied, believing in his faith and hope. Then, he kissed me.

CHAPTER TWELVE

Levi decided he wanted to grill hamburgers despite the snow. He fired up the grill while Winnie helped me in the kitchen.

"Momma, can Soraya come over tonight?" she asked.

"Sure. I don't see why not," I replied.

"May I call her?" she asked.

"Sure, just let me talk to Betty. Okay?"

She rushed to the living room to find my phone. Aydan appeared in the kitchen from the garage. He and Callum decided to change the oil in the Camaro. They ended up having to call Troy for advice. When Levi and I came in, I could hear them video chatting with him through their phone.

"Get it finished?" I asked him. He wiped his greasy hands on a blue towel and nodded.

"It was harder than I thought it would be, but I think we could do it again quicker," he said.

"Good. I expect you to keep it in shape. Your father loved that car."

"I love it, too. But I want to make sure it's still in good shape whenever Winnie gets old enough to drive," he said.

"You are a sweetheart. You didn't get that from me."

"I must have gotten it from Dad," he said.

"Maybe," I replied, as Winnie handed me the phone.

"Here, Momma. It's Mrs. Betty."

I dried off my hands and answered.

"Howdy."

"Are you sure you want another kid in the house?" Betty asked.

"Sure. What's one more? I lost count after two," I teased just as Callum appeared at the back door.

"Hey, I heard that," he said with a smile.

"If you are sure, I'll have Luther bring her over," Betty said.

"We are just about to start dinner. She can eat with us," I offered.

"Sounds great. I appreciate this, Grace. She's a lot younger than us, and she seems to have a never-ending well of energy."

"Winnie does too. We will have fun," I said.

"Alright. See you soon. Oh, and we are going to open the diner tomorrow," she said.

"Sounds great!"

I handed the phone back to Winnie. "I can't wait until she gets here."

"Is your room cleaned up?" I asked.

"I'll go see," she said, trotting off up the stairs in a hurry. I knew that it was cleaned up and that she never had to do it. One of benefits of having brownies in the house. They did keep things tidy.

Levi appeared from the back porch. "The grill is ready. Where are the patties?"

"I'm finishing them up," I replied.

"Need help?"

"No."

"Good. I didn't want to help you anyway," he teased. "How's the car? Y'all get it put back together?"

"We did," Callum said. "You could have helped us."

"If it was a tractor, then I'm your man, but I don't fix cars," Levi explained.

"Farmer boy," I muttered.

"Fairy wench," he returned.

"What!?"

Aydan and Callum snickered, as Levi ducked around a corner. I looked for something to throw at him, but had to settle for an evil look.

"I'm going to freeze your balls off," I said.

"Whoa, whoa, whoa. Don't mess with the goods, Glory. You might need them later," he teased from behind the wall.

"Are you scared, Dublin?"

"Yes, ma'am," he replied with a deep Texas twang.

"Get these burgers on the grill," I demanded.

He scooted past me, grabbing the plate of patties, then smacked me on the butt. I know I turned twenty shades of red.

"Oops. My hand slipped," he said, then ducked out the back door.

"You can sleep on the porch for all I care!" I yelled at him.

"You guys are fun," Callum said. "My parents were never like that."

"Like what?" I asked.

"Happy," he said.

"Killjoy," Aydan muttered.

Callum shoved him on the shoulder, but I saw the hurt in his eyes. "You don't talk about them often," I said.

"Nope. Nothing to talk about. They are gone," he said. "I'm sorry to dampen the spirits."

I gathered him up in my arms and hugged his slender but strong frame. "You are home now," I said.

He hugged me back. "Thanks, Mom."

SORAYA JOINED us just before dinner. Her frame was thicker than Winnie's slender one. She had striking cornflower blue eyes and jet-black hair. When she smiled, her eyes twinkled to a silver color. She was sweet and polite, and it seemed like she and Winnie had hit it off pretty well.

"Soraya, where do you live?" I asked.

"With Gramps and Betty," she replied.

"Oh, you have moved to Shady Grove? Where are your parents?" I asked.

Her eyes darkened, and she shrugged. I'd dug a hole that I couldn't get out of.

"I'm glad she is here," Winnie piped up, saving me from an embarrassing conversation.

"Me too. You can spend the night anytime, Soraya," I said.

"My friends call me Raya," she said finally smiling again.

"Raya, it is," I replied.

"*Thank your daughter for the save on that one,*" Levi said.

"*How was I supposed to know that her parents weren't here? I hate it. She's adorable,*" I said.

"*Grace, you can't save every child.*"

"*Not all of them, but I'll step up if needed.*"

"*I'm sure Luther and Betty have this one covered.*"

"*Yes. I'm sure.*"

After dessert, we cleared the table and Aydan took out some board games to play. We had nothing better to do, and it was nice to have the family all together. Just as we had sat down to the coffee table in the living room, the power went out. The room turned cold and dark very quickly.

"It's just the electricity," Levi said. "Let me call Tennyson."

Winnie lifted her hand and said, "Fire."

A small ball of flame appeared above her hand which lit the room in a warm glow. My insides panicked, but outwardly I tried to show confidence.

"Aydan, find some candles while Winnie and I light the fire-place," I instructed.

"Yes, ma'am," he said jumping up from his seat. His eyes were wide and watching Winnie closely.

"Come here, sweetheart," I coaxed her to the fireplace. She watched the ball in her hand as she steadily walked toward me. The ball didn't waver or die out. I arranged the wood in the fireplace quickly placing kindling where she could put her fire.

"Want me to throw it in there?" she asked.

"I would prefer if you just handed it over," I replied.

"Okay," she said, then leaned down to ignite the wood.

It blazed up, warming the room and providing light. Aydan returned with candles and a lighter. He placed them around the room, refusing Winnie's offer to light the candles too.

"You did a great job, Winnie."

"Thank you, Momma."

"She's been doing a lot better with my Gramp teaching her," Raya said.

"I can see. Very impressive."

"Except when she gets cold," Raya added.

"It doesn't happen much," Winnie said.

"You will tell me next time it happens, right?" I reminded her.

"Yes, ma'am," she said.

Levi spoke to Tennyson in the kitchen just outside of my scope of hearing with all the kids chatting in the room. I joined him in the darkness.

"Alright. As long as everyone is okay," Levi said. "Let me know if you need my help."

He disconnected the call.

"Well?" I asked.

"The squirrels attacked the power station just outside of town, but inside the ward. The lines fried the squirrels that attacked, but the power is out. Tennyson has someone coming to fix it," he said.

"So, we play games in the dark," I said.

"I'm worried it's an attack," Levi said.

"The ward is fine?"

"Yes."

"Then relax and enjoy some time with your family."

He kissed me on the cheek. "Winnie and the fire ball, eh?"

"It was impressive and controlled."

"She will master it before long."

"Then what do we do with her?"

"I have no idea," he laughed. "But for now, I'm going to kick your ass in Monopoly."

~

Since the power didn't come back on, we camped out in the living room with blankets and pillows. Levi and I took the couch while Aydan slept in the recliner. Winnie and Soraya curled up next to each other under the same blanket, and Callum left after Monopoly to check on Troy, Amanda, and the wolves.

Levi stroked my hair idly as I dozed off using his chest as a pillow.

The dream started. A nightmare.

I stood in the coldest part of the Winter realm. My father stood behind me and his witch bound my powers. Across from us, a man stood tall with his chin lifted in defiance. His hands were bound behind his back, and his back and torso bore the scars of a recent whipping.

"This matter is brought before the Winter court," a dark-haired man wearing a hood, and standing beside the accused said. His voice echoed in my father's Hall of Judgment.

"Recite the charges," Oberon said.

"Treason. Dishonor to the Great Sword. Dishonor to the daughter of the King," the hooded man said.

I tried to protest the last one, because I was a willing participant in everything that we had done. My mouth moved, but no sound came out.

"Easy, my child. It shall be over soon," my father said.

"His verdict is guilty by the council of the King," the man called out to the room of witnesses. A low murmur spread across the room.

Mercy! I wanted to scream. Mercy! I pulled power, only to have it squashed by the witch. Tears rolled down my cheeks as I watched my lover stand before the executioner.

"What is his sentence, Brother?" a man to my left asked. Through my blurry tears, I could see his face. My uncle. Brockton.

"He is forsaken," Oberon answered.

"No!" I managed to scream through the magic. My voice resounded against the walls like shattering glass, then quickly died away. The witnesses to this act would remember my resonant refusal to accept this verdict.

"Proceed," my father ordered.

I could not say his name. He was forsaken. He continued to hold his head high, but his denim blue eyes pierced through me like daggers. A smile stretched across his face. As the executioner dragged a sharp blade across his neck, he mouthed the words, "I will love you forever."

His blood poured from his neck, staining the snow-white floors of the hall. An innocent man killed because he loved the wrong woman.

"Bring me the sword," my father said. The executioner sheathed his dagger, then picked up the Great Sword beside him. He walked to my father holding it up with two hands, then bowed before him to present it. "Finally, Excalibur has returned to me."

"What about your daughter?" a woman asked.

When I lifted my watery eyes, I saw the Queen of Summer standing to the side.

"What about her? She was manipulated in this. Surely you see that," Oberon protested.

"I see a broken-hearted woman who pleaded through the heaviest magic for a man she was forbidden to love! I know she is your favorite, Oberon, but you must deal with it," she insisted.

I felt the magical bonds release me. Rushing across the room, I knelt beside the bleeding body of my lover. His face was covered by his dark brown hair. The lights in the room reflected on it revealing touches of copper.

"Gloriana, daughter of...my daughter, you are exiled from the Otherworld until the day you die," Oberon said.

I focused on the dead man before me. The guards were rushing up to take me away. Reaching out to the strands of hair blocking his face, I pushed them away.

"Levi? Oh no, this isn't right! Levi! Levi! Wake up! No, this isn't how it happened. No!" I screamed in a fit waking up the entire house.

Levi hovered over me holding my arms still.

"Grace! Wake up. Look at me!" he insisted.

"Is she okay?" Winnie whimpered.

"Winnie, come here," Aydan said. "You, too, Soraya."

They scampered across the room, climbing up into the recliner with him. Winnie buried her face in his chest, and Soraya stared at Levi and me.

My heart pounded, and I couldn't catch my breath. "It wasn't you," I said.

"I'm right here," he replied. "What the hell was that?"

"A nightmare."

"Yeah, I got that part." He released my hands, and I reached up to touch his face.

"It was the day I was exiled," I explained.

"Just calm down, and you can tell me about it when you are ready," he said, but he clearly wanted to know more. His blue eyes reflected the flames of the fire.

"There was a man that I loved. He was forsaken, and I was banished," I explained as shortly as possible.

"They killed him?"

"Yes, but for some reason, in the dream, it wasn't him. It was you," I choked out.

"Did he look like me?"

"No. You are very different from him. I don't know why you were there. It's an omen," I muttered.

"Nonsense. Grace, it was a bad dream. That's all," he said, refusing to believe it was more. It was a memory. It felt real up until the point that I saw Levi's face instead of the man I once loved. "You want some water? Can I get you anything?"

"No."

"Someone is coming," Levi said, jumping up from the couch. Rufus began to bark loudly. Levi ran to the front door, opened it, and Callum came rushing through it in a ball of white fur. He exploded into his human form causing Rufus to scamper away.

"You need to come quickly," he huffed, trying to catch his breath.

"Squirrels?" I asked.

"Yeti?" Levi questioned.

"No, Amanda is in labor, and we can't find Tabitha. Troy asked for you to come," Callum explained.

"Sure. Aydan, stay with the girls," I instructed, forgetting about the dream. I jumped up from the couch and ran to gather clothes in the laundry room. "Callum, run to the RV camp and find Wendy. I'm sure the gypsies have a midwife."

"Yes, ma'am," he said, then shifted to his white wolf. He bounded out of the door, and Levi closed it behind him.

"Have Bramble and Briar recovered?" Levi asked.

"We are here, my King," Bramble said from the coffee table.

Briar and Thistle stood beside him. "With headaches, but yes, we are here," Briar added.

"The first sign of trouble you come and get us," Levi instructed.

Bramble clicked his heels, saluted, but bopped himself in the head. "Ow! Yes, Sir."

"Aydan, the safest place outside of the house is the circle or the vault," I said.

"Mom, it's going to be fine. Go help Amanda," he assured me.

Just before we rushed out of the door, I leaned over and kissed each one of them on the forehead. "I love you. Even you, little Raya."

"Thank you, my Queen," she said with a blush.

"Love you, Momma," Winnie said. She managed a weak smile.

"Grace, let's go," Levi said. He grabbed my hand, pulling me over to him. "Are you okay?"

"There are more important things. We can discuss it later," I said.

Levi lifted Excalibur. It glowed with Winter Blue power as he swung it in a circle opening the portal to Troy's house which I could see through the glittering haze. We walked through, and he closed the portal behind us.

CHAPTER THIRTEEN

AFTER PORTING INTO THE MAYNARDS' FRONT YARD, WE SPRINTED UP the steps to the Capps' home, and Levi knocked on the door.

"It's us!' he yelled.

"Come in!" Troy called out.

The door opened, and a wide-eyed Mark greeted us. "Come in. They are upstairs," he said, pointing to the steps behind him. The howls of Amanda in labor filled the house.

I touched Mark's face. "It will be okay."

He nodded in response, as Levi rushed up the stairs toward the noise. I followed closely behind him. A woman knelt beside Amanda, wiping her forehead with a damp cloth. Candles littered the room to give it more light. Two large oil lamps sat near the end of the bed.

"Midwife?" I asked.

"No. I'm just the pack nurse," she said. "But I need help."

"Alright. I've done this before, tell me what you need me to do," I said.

"You've delivered a baby?" Levi asked.

"Honey, when you live as long as I have, you have done it all," I said with confidence.

"She's in too much pain. There is a complication. I hoped to have a doctor consult," the woman said.

"Grace, this is Artemis," Troy said, then turned his focus back to comforting Amanda.

Her body became rigid, and she screamed through a contraction.

"Seems pretty normal," I said, reaching out to grasp her hand.

"There are three," Artemis said.

"Triplets?" Levi asked.

"Wolves have litters," Troy muttered. "Only she can't have them as a wolf. That's why I'm here. I have to keep her from shifting with the pain."

"Was Mark an only child?" I asked.

"Not the time, Grace," Levi scolded.

"Sorry," I muttered. "One or three, the object is the same. Let's get them out."

Levi's guitar started to play a soothing tune that sounded like a lullaby. Amanda immediately relaxed, as did Troy. I sat down at the base of the chair where Amanda was seated and lifted up her skirt. The truth was, I'd only helped with a couple of births. Childbirth, no matter what they say, isn't pretty. What I saw surprised me. A little booty pressing out of her body.

"Well, the first one is a girl," I said. "The bad news is she is breech."

"I'm here," Wendy said behind me as she arrived. "Oh, my!"

"Are you the midwife?" I asked.

"Yep. We need to get her on her knees. It will make the breech easier for her," Wendy explained.

"No, we can't do that," Troy exclaimed. "It's hard enough to keep her from shifting like this than to keep her in check doggystyle!"

"Well, you are just going to have to alpha harder," I said. He snarled at me. It was rather intimidating. Levi's song changed slightly as Troy's anxieties rose. Wendy put her hand on his shoulder.

"We are going to take good care of her and your children," Wendy said, trying to calm him down.

As Wendy and I helped her move, I caught a glimpse of Mark standing in the hallway peeking into the room. Artemis gathered towels and the supplies that we would need.

"*Levi, can you play from the hallway?*"

Levi lifted his head to see the boy. "*Got it,*" he replied, then moved to the hallway. "Come here, Mark. I'll show you how my guitar works." Levi led the boy away from the door so we could work without distraction.

Once we got Amanda in position, she groaned as another contraction bore down on her body. Her muscles tightened as the pain ripped through her. Troy spoke softly in her ear. Through my sight I could see a warm amber glow flowing from him to her.

"When it comes, push," Wendy said.

"Okay," she whimpered.

The contraction hit her hard, and she screamed, splitting the muffled tones we had previously used. Troy held her shoulders tightly.

"Push!" Wendy commanded.

I reached forward to brace the little bottom that now protruded from her body. Another contraction came, and another. We repeated the process until the completely breeched girl slid out into my hands. I took her little body to the side, as Amanda continued to contract. I used a towel that Troy had to clean her face. Most babies I'd seen come into the world screaming, but this one was quiet. The mother was doing all the lung work.

Thankfully, the second one came out head first and with only two pushes. I laid her next to her sister, wiping off her little purplish body. Her limbs jerked about with the sudden change of temperature and surroundings.

"Are they okay?" Amanda cried.

"They are beautiful," I assured her.

"One more time, Amanda. You can do this," Wendy said.

"That's right, Wife. You've got this," Troy assured her.

The last contraction was more of a whimper than anything, and the last little girl came into this world in the normal way, screaming at the top of her lungs. I heard shuffling behind us. I turned to find Levi, holding Mark back.

"What did you do to her?" Mark demanded.

"She's fine," I said with the small screaming baby in my arms. "They are all fine."

"She's crying! Did you hurt her?" His lips turned up on the side revealing his sharp canines.

Amanda rolled over on her side, and Wendy promptly covered her with a blanket. Troy released Amanda's hand to reach out to Mark.

"Son, come here. Your mother and your new sisters are doing just fine. Wendy, Artemis, and Grace are helping us," Troy told him.

Levi let him go, and he sprinted to his father. He kept his eyes on Wendy who produced needle, thread, and scissors to cut the cords. I helped her prep the area to try to prevent any kind of infection. It was something I'd learned while traveling with the gypsies. We had many births in the wagon train.

"Good, Grace. You have done this before," Wendy said with a smile.

"A time or two," I admitted.

"Where is Tab?" I asked, looking at Levi.

"Can't you feel her?" Levi asked.

"Yes, but I think she is out of town," I said.

"What?" Levi prodded.

"She's busy," I replied.

"Oh!" Levi said, recognizing what I had felt.

"We don't need her," Wendy said. "Amanda is doing fine considering the strain. Wolf mothers are always resilient."

"You've delivered wolves before?" I asked.

"Yes. Wolves, bears, rabbits, and deer," Wendy explained.

"Wow! That's impressive," I replied in awe.

"Thanks," she smiled as she worked on sewing up the umbilical cords. As she finished them, I handed the babies to Amanda and Troy. Mark stood beside his father with his focus on Wendy.

Levi helped me clean up the mess as the family adored their new additions.

"What are their names?" Levi asked.

"The oldest is Rosalie, then Magnolia, and the loud one is Camilla," Amanda said.

"And they are *my* sisters," Mark added.

"*Well, there's a little alpha for you,*" I said to Levi.

"*Maybe all he needed was a reason,*" Levi replied.

"*Three reasons,*" I added.

"They are beautiful," I said, stepping forward. I lifted my hand and three tiny snowflakes appeared. "As the Queen of this realm, I offer a blessing of protection and hope for all three of your lovely daughters." I blew across my palm, and a snowflake landed on each head quickly melting to a dot of water.

"Thank you, Grace," Troy said. I saw tears hovering at the edges of his eyes.

Levi and I slipped out quietly as Wendy and Artemis discussed the birth quietly away from the family at the back side of the room. I entered the bathroom in the hallway to wash my hands.

"You were amazing in there," Levi said. "I have to admit that it looks very different than the video they showed us in school."

"They show you a real video of a birth in school? Heathens!" I exclaimed.

"Shh!" Levi warned, laughing.

"You were there when Aydan was born," I said.

"Yes, but I didn't look," he replied. "I was trying not to look at Amanda out of respect and privacy, but Mark is quick. I didn't expect him to dart back into the room."

I dried my hands off on a towel, then put my arms around Levi's neck.

"If you want children, I won't deny you," I said.

"Grace, I don't know what I want," he admitted.

"Me?" I asked.

"That's a given," he replied, as he pressed me closer to him. It was definitely a given.

"Whatever you decide is fine with me," I replied.

"After the war," he said. My mind flashed back to the dream, and I tried to pull away from him, but he wouldn't let me. "Grace?"

"Um, yeah, sorry. Just hot in here," I replied.

"You are never hot. Good try, but not good enough," he scolded. He leaned forward touching my forehead with his. "Talk to me."

"The dream flashed through my head," I replied.

"We seem to have dream issues." He was trying to make light of it.

I took a deep breath, then let it out slowly. "Yeah, I prefer the other one."

"So do I. What a coincidence." He smiled. "Grace, we cannot fear what we do not know for sure. We can only prepare for what might come. And I'll tell you right now, if I died today, I'd die happier than I've ever been, because I know your heart belongs to me."

"But we haven't…"

"Does that determine your heart?"

"Of course it doesn't," I replied.

"Then, what does it matter?"

"It would just be disappointing not to get to, I mean, just once," I explained. Laughter danced in his eyes as he enjoyed my discomfort with the conversation.

"Once is not going to be enough."

"I hope not."

Callum appeared in the doorway behind Levi.

"Hey, I want to show you something," Callum said, then looked back and forth at us. "Oh, sorry to interrupt."

"No problem. What ya got?" Levi asked, turning his back on me.

"Come here," he said. We followed him to the doorway where the newly expanded family gushed over the babies. "Look at Mark with your sight."

I opened my sight and was astounded. In place of the young boy, a tall, lean, and muscular man stood with determination in his eyes. An amber glow surrounded him. His jaw was set in fierce determination, but there was also a gentleness to his stance.

"What is it?" I whispered.

"Wow," Levi added.

"His alpha characteristics have emerged. I suppose having three helpless sisters provoked it," Callum explained. "It's pretty awesome."

"Yes, it is," I said. Troy made eye contact with me, and my sight shifted to him. He had the same look about him in the magical spectrum. The same amber glow. He looked proudly upon his children, especially Mark.

Out of the corner of my eye, I caught movement at the top of the steps. Dominick stood there. I tried to decipher his facial expression. There was relief, pain, longing, and a strength I couldn't define.

I moved away from Levi and Callum. *"Give me a minute."*

"Sure," Levi replied.

"Hey," I whispered to him.

"Is she okay?" he asked.

"She's fine. A proud mother of three baby girls," I said.

"Mark?" he asked.

"He's changed," I replied.

"Oh," he said.

"That doesn't change things for you though does it?" I asked.

"Just means that from now on Troy is obligated to focus on his son's development as the next alpha for the pack," he said. "I'm happy for them."

He turned to leave, but I reached out and grabbed his arm. "Wait, Nick. Are you okay?"

"Yeah, sure. I'm going to go tell the pack that everything is fine. The power will be back on soon," he said. "The workers were finishing up when I headed back here."

"Nick," I pushed.

"Not now, Grace. Maybe later," he said. I released him and watched him walk away. He had so many doubts about his place here. Finding him a solution for his hand was even more important now. He would never be the Alpha of the Shady Grove pack, and despite his initial desire to renounce his Alpha status, it clearly still meant something to him.

Levi embraced me from behind. "It has to be hard for him," he said.

"I want to go home," I replied.

"Alright. I'll tell Troy we are leaving," he said, kissing the top of my head. He released me to go and speak to Troy.

"I'm gonna stay here tonight, Mom," Callum said. "Just in case they need anything. Kiss Winnie goodnight for me. Tell Aydan I'll see him in the morning."

I placed my hand on his cheek. "Of course, try to get some rest, too."

"I will," he said, hugging me tightly.

When Levi and I arrived home, Winnie and Raya were curled up together back on the floor with their blanket. Not far away, Aydan slept. His eyes fluttered with our arrival. I motioned for him to go back to sleep. I felt exhausted after the excitement at Troy's house. Levi sensed it, tugging me to the couch. We resumed our previous positions and quickly fell asleep.

CHAPTER FOURTEEN

WINNIE SAT ON THE COUCH EATING CINNAMON ROLLS WHILE watching television with Soraya. "Mom, where is Callum?"

"He's out with the wolves. Mrs. Maynard had her babies. Three little girls. I think Callum is helping with them since Troy is busy," I explained.

"Three babies? How's Mark?" she asked.

"He loves his sisters," I replied.

"Sisters? All three?"

"Yes, ma'am. Three pretty little flowers," I said. "The Maynards named them after flowers."

"Callum isn't my brother," she said.

I stopped cleaning up in the kitchen and looked at her. She wasn't looking at me. I assumed she had said it to Soraya who cut her eyes to me and back. Perhaps the little girl had a crush on him.

"No, he's not technically, but he is part of the family," I said.

"Uncle Levi isn't my uncle," she added.

"No, he's not," I said. "Winnie, what are you getting at?"

"Nothing," she said.

"I don't believe you," I said.

"She has a crush on him," Aydan said.

"Aydan!" she fussed. "I do not! Take it back!"

"Whoa, now. That's enough of that yelling. We have a guest and we aren't going to act like heathens," I said, invoking the mom voice.

"Sorry," she muttered. "Aydan, it's not nice to tell secrets."

"I'm sorry, Winnie," he said.

"Winnie has a crush on Callum," I told Levi who was across town at the trailer.

"Yeah?"

"You knew?"

"Um, yeah."

"I must be blind."

"You are her mother. You don't think about her or him that way, but yes, she's been staring at him. It's puppy love, and I assure you, he knows, too."

"Damn. Okay," I replied. I was disappointed in my parenting skills not to notice that my daughter had a crush on my, sort of, adopted son.

"I'm sorry, Mom," Aydan said, bringing me out of my self-inspection.

"It's okay. I guess I didn't notice," I said.

"I think it's a new thing," he said. "Callum noticed."

"Levi said that he probably knew," I admitted.

"It's funny that you can talk to him like that," he said.

"We can talk like that, too. I can teach you how," I said. "You have a lot of gifts from your father, but I've got to think there is a little of me in there."

"I know what Winnie means by being cold. I feel that too sometimes," he said.

"I'm so used to it that I don't even realize it," I said.

"You will teach me to use the magic?" he asked.

"Of course," I replied.

"Good. I want to learn, because when you go to fight, I want to go with you," he said.

"Aydan, I need you to stay here and protect your sister," I said.

"I want to go with you," he whined. "Winnie is learning to use her powers. She might be able to go too."

"No! Your father gave his life for her. He would have done the same for you. I can't put you in the middle of that fight. We have to respect his sacrifice," I said with tears welling up in my eyes. "I can't lose you, too."

"Mom," he said, then hugged me. "You're right. I'm sorry. I swear to protect Winnie."

"You are such a good boy. I love you, Aydan," I said. "Come with me."

He followed me upstairs to my bedroom. I opened the closet door that should have been his father's. Inside it, a leather jacket hung from a hanger. I took it off and handed it to him.

"Dad's?" he asked.

"Yes. It has always been a comfort to me, but you should have it," I said. "He would want you to have it."

"What about Winnie?" he asked.

"When she gets bigger, I have something for her, too," I replied. "Put it on."

He pushed his hands through the sleeves which were just a touch too long. He would grow into it. It was striking how much he looked like his father. I couldn't hold back the tears.

"Don't cry, Mom," he said, hugging me tightly. The scent of leather and mint almost knocked me over. The memories of his father rushed over me.

"He would be so proud of you."

"Thank you for giving it to me. I promise to take good care of it," he said.

I wiped my eyes and smiled at my son. Before we went downstairs, Aydan hung the jacket in his closet. He didn't want Winnie to see the jacket. She would know it belonged to Dylan. When we returned downstairs, we overheard Winnie talking to Raya.

"I want a big girl room," Winnie said.

"I love your room," Soraya said.

"Don't you think it's too little girlish?" Winnie asked.

"No, I think it's perfect," Soraya answered. "I've never had a room like that. My grandparents said I could do my room however I wanted though. Want to help me decorate it?"

"That sounds like fun!" Winnie said. I hoped she realized that not every little girl out there was lucky enough to have parents who gave her just about everything she wanted. She clearly couldn't remember those days at her mother's trailer when she barely had anything. I hoped she never knew those kinds of days ever again, but she also needed to learn to be respectful of others.

After cleaning the kitchen, Winnie asked if we could go and visit Troy and Amanda. I called over there, and Callum said that it would be fine. We loaded up the truck and headed to wolf head-quarters.

When we arrived, it seemed there were several folks there from in town to see the new babies. Astor and Ella exited as we walked up the steps.

"Mornin' Ella. How are you feeling?" I asked.

"Ready for mine to come too! I thought maybe if I came over here and let my little ones hear the new baby sounds, it might encourage them to make an appearance," she said.

"I don't think it works that way," I replied.

"No, it doesn't. But I can hope. I'm huge!" she said, rubbing her belly.

"You are beautiful," Astor said.

Ella smiled and ran her fingers through his beard. "Thank you, my Love," she said. "Any squirrel problems at your house?"

"No, I think my brownie brigade is keeping them clear," I replied.

"Send them to our house. I know there are five or six inside," she said.

"In the attic?" I asked.

"No, they are in the house. It's driving me nuts," she said.

"Nuts," Aydan giggled.

"He has his father's sense of humor," I said.

"Do I?" Aydan asked.

"Yes. Lord knows I wouldn't laugh at such a thing," I replied.

"Then why are you smiling?" he asked.

"Hush your mouth and get in that house," I said, pointing at the door. He laughed, but he along with Winnie and Soraya ran into the house. Mark met them at the door, and he grabbed Winnie's hand.

"Come with me," he said rather forcefully for a young fella. That big alpha inside of him was already commanding my daughter around. I'd have to keep an eye on that.

"He's changed overnight," Astor said.

"Yes, but he's not going to order my daughter around," I said.

"Grace, she is too much like you. She won't let it happen," Ella said.

"Good for her! Y'all be safe, and I'll send Bramble over to help with the squirrels. Maybe it's Rufus that keeps them out. If Bramble doesn't work, I'll send the dog," I replied.

"Have a good day, Grace," Astor said, as he helped Ella down the steps.

"You, too," I replied, then went inside.

AT THE TOP of the steps, I peeked into the room to see Mark hovering over a crib with three sleeping babies. Amanda was also asleep on the bed. Troy noticed me from his seat next to her and came over to meet me.

"How was the first night?" I asked.

"Tiresome. Camilla is a screamer," he said. "They are wonderful though. I never thought I could ever love like this. Before you came to town, I was happy to be a lone wolf and sheriff. Now I have a family."

"You were an idiot about not wanting those kids," I said.

He grinned. "Yes, I was." Proud papa. "I don't know if I was more of an idiot over the babies or Mark. Can you see the change?"

"I saw it last night through my sight. I can see the man he is going to be," I said.

"You can?"

"Yes, he'll be handsome, strong, but with a gentle, steady spirit," I said.

"Exactly what a pack needs," Troy said. "Unless one of the girls beats him to it."

"Ever seen any female-led packs?" I asked.

"Occasionally. They are rare, but there are matriarchal packs," he said.

"What about Dominick?" I asked.

"He's still my second. I'll need him more than ever while I train Mark. It will be his job to watch over the pack for me when I'm busy," Troy explained.

"Then you should probably reassure him of his place. He looked sad last night. Even though he's renounced his alpha side, it doesn't mean that he has forgotten that part of himself. I assume there is a part of him that still longs to hold that role," I said.

"Really? Assuming is bad, Grace," Troy teased.

"I assume based on my own suppressed desires to rule," I said.

"Oh, well, in that case, I'd say it wasn't assuming at all. I worry about my children in this war," Troy said, looking back to his daughters.

"We all do. Seeing that they are safe is the top priority going forward. Our children shouldn't suffer for our actions," I said.

"You have. You are suffering because your father allowed Rhiannon and his council to banish his daughter," he said with a twinge of hatred in his voice.

"I wasn't innocent," I replied, watching Winnie and Mark. She eyed him curiously. I wondered if she could see him through her sight. We hadn't talked about fairy sight, but it would be a conversation that we needed to have soon.

"He was your father," Troy said.

"I know that when he left this world, he was sorry for what happened. I also know that in his own way he loved me. There are those who don't even have that," I said.

"Like Dominick. And Amanda," he said.

"And you," I added.

"And me," he agreed. "Mark, why don't you go play with Winnie?"

"I need to protect my sisters," he said.

"Mark, I'm here with them. Your mother and I will protect them," Troy said.

"Okay," Mark replied reluctantly.

Mark walked out of the room with Winnie on his heels. "Mom, can I stay and play here today?"

"It's up to Mark's daddy," I said.

"I'll be up here," Mark said.

Callum appeared around the corner. "I'll keep an eye on them," he said.

"Hey. How are you this morning?" I asked.

"I'm good, Mom," he said. "Morning, Aydan."

"Hey, man," Aydan replied.

"Come on. Let's go watch the kids," Callum coaxed.

"Alright," Aydan said.

"Try to get some rest. Let us know if there is anything we can do," I said.

"Thanks, Grace," Troy replied before returning to his watchpost between the beds of his family.

When I got downstairs, Mark and Winnie were on the floor playing with building blocks. The kind that hurt like the dickens if you step on them. Aydan and Callum were playing video games. Usually, Winnie watched Callum, but she was intently watching Mark. She had to see that he was different. If it wasn't her sight, she was picking up on it with her senses.

"Can you come to the office?" Levi asked.

"Of course," I replied.

Gathering power, I focused on Levi and skipped to the trailer. When I entered my office, he was sitting at my desk and Tennyson was poised in his chair.

"Morning, Grace," Tennyson said.

"Mornin'," I replied, before taking a seat on the couch across from my desk.

"You want your seat?" Levi asked.

"Nope, I'm good. What's going on?" I asked.

"You can't kill Stephanie," Tennyson said. He leaned back in his chair to gauge my response.

"Why the fuck not?" I asked.

"The helmet is tied to the veil, and it is tied to her," Tennyson said. "It doesn't matter if it's on her head or not. She has to live or she has to give it to you or Levi."

"She's not going to give it to me," I said, looking at Levi.

"She says she will give it to me if she and I..."

"Hell, fucking, no," I said. Tennyson chuckled. "It's not funny, asshat."

"I'm not laughing at you, Grace. I'm amused by your fire. For one so cold, you have it in abundance," he explained.

"Fuck off," I said.

"That's three fucks in one small conversation. I think that's enough," Levi said.

"Since when do you count my fucks?" I snarled.

"When they aren't with me," he replied. Tennyson laughed again.

"Shut up, Lachlan," I huffed.

I felt someone else approaching the trailer. It was Finley. He strutted in the room like the arrogant fool that he was.

"Hello everyone," he said. He leaned over and kissed me on the cheek. "Glory."

"Fin," I replied.

"So, what has you all riled up?" he asked.

"I am not riled up!" I replied.

"I love you, Sister, but you are a terrible liar," Finley joked.

"Why are you here?" I asked.

"To give you a hard time," he replied.

"That's my job," Levi said.

"You aren't doing it," Finley replied. The room became very silent.

"Why are you so obsessed with whether or not Levi and I are fucking?" I asked.

"Four," Levi said.

"Levi Rearden," I warned.

He put his hand over his mouth and tried not to laugh.

"Because, the longer it goes the more sexasperated you get," Finley said.

"Do I even want to know what that is?" I asked.

"Probably not, but I'm going to tell you anyway. It's like hangry," he said.

"Hangry?"

"So hungry you are angry. Which makes you exasperated with the lack of sex."

"More like exasperating," Levi said.

"I am going to jerk you bald!"

Tennyson was rolling by this point, and it just frustrated me more. Finley was right. I needed to get laid.

"Jerk away, sweetheart." Levi managed to say through his laughing.

"We have probably pushed our limits here, gentlemen," Tennyson said, trying to defuse the situation.

"Probably so. Sorry, Glory," Finley said.

"I'm not," Levi replied. I showed him my middle finger. "Promises, promises."

"What about the damn helmet!?" I exclaimed.

Tennyson gathered his composure to answer my question. "It seems that we were correct in assuming the helmet is tied to the veil. It is also tied to Stephanie since she put it on. Brockton played us in the Otherworld, hoping you would destroy the veil. It would discredit you to everyone here and you would lose whatever royal power you have left. Instead, we were wise not to destroy Stephanie right away. She will have to give the helmet up or wear it until her death. If she dies by natural causes, the first person that puts it on will take on its power. If she is killed, then the veil between the human world and the fairy world will fall."

"Son of a bitch," Finley muttered.

"Or she can give it to me," Levi said.

"No," I said. "For now, she lives. Why wouldn't Brockton come after her here? His plan to discredit me failed. Why would he wait to kill her?"

"His attack at trailer swamp didn't work. I doubt he has

anything else for now to renew that attack. We hold Shady Grove, and there is nothing he can do about it," Tennyson explained.

"So, the bitch gets to live," I said.

"For now," Tennyson replied.

"Well, fuck," I said, then quickly covered my mouth.

Levi's eyes sparkled. "Five."

CHAPTER FIFTEEN

I PICKED UP WINNIE AND SORAYA BEFORE GOING HOME. LUTHER MET us at the house to take his granddaughter. He helped her into his pickup, then approached me. I saw the look in his eyes. He wanted to talk.

"Winnie, run inside and make sure Rufus has been fed. Then you can help me with dinner," I said.

She waved goodbye to Soraya and took off running.

"Thank you for having her, Grace," Luther said.

"I won't pry, but she seems a bit sad," I said.

"My children are all over this earth. Some are good. Some are bad. Her parents in particular are very bad. That's why I have her training with Zahir. I don't want her to follow their path," he said.

"Are they dead?" I asked.

"Beings like us don't really die. We just pass from one existence to the next, but in a way, for her, they are dead," he said. "They are in that world in between waiting for their fate to be decided. Zahir is keeping her out of that realm until they are gone," he said.

"I'm not familiar with your ways. What happened to them?" I asked.

"They turned to darkness. I suppose it is my own fault. I took that route myself. Betty has tempered my fire," he said.

"I understand that. Dylan melted my cold. Levi tempers it," I said.

"We need the tempered queen, not the melted one. You will need that coldness for what is ahead," he replied. "When I moved to Shady Grove, Jeremiah promised that my darkness would fade, and it has. For you, it has been the same. However, for the fight ahead, we must embrace our darkness, knowing it does not rule us."

I hadn't thought of it that way. Dylan's effect on me suppressed the cold almost completely. With Levi, I can use it, but I know if it goes too far, he will bring me back. "I know. Soraya is welcome to visit anytime. I spoke to Troy earlier. Our next priority is to make sure our children are safe. If you have any input, I welcome it. With Astor and Ella due soon, we will have plenty of children to keep safe during the war," I said.

"I will think on it. We need to be preparing them as well for the inevitability that they will have to protect themselves. Most of them have powers to do so. We should encourage them," he said.

"Winnie is doing so much better. I can't thank you enough for what you've done with her. She lit the fire the other night when the power went out," I said.

"Yes, but the cold is being suppressed. I'm afraid if she can't learn to balance them, she will always be a bit of a wildcard," he said.

"Sometimes you need a wildcard in the deck," I said.

"Sometimes you do," he said with a smile. "Goodnight, Grace."

"Night," I replied.

When I walked back into the house, Winnie waylaid me with questions. "Momma, what happened to Mark? Why does he look old?"

"Winnie, you can see the man behind the boy?" I asked.

"Yes, he's old," she repeated.

"That's Mark's aura. His alpha tendencies have emerged. One day, he will grow up to be the man you can see," I explained.

She put down the water bowl for Rufus, then proceeded to

dump food into his food bowl. He stood below her wagging his tail in anticipation.

"How do I see that?" she asked.

"It's part of your fairy side," I said.

"Part of what you gave me?"

"Yes."

"You can see him too?"

"I can, plus lots of other things. I'm surprised your sight has developed. I'll teach you how to use it. It can be turned on and off."

"What about the cold, Momma?"

"What about it?"

"I don't know what to do with it." She walked over to me, and we sat together on the couch.

"Baby, you will figure it out. It just takes time. You have plenty of time. I don't want you to grow up too fast."

"Like Aydan."

"Like Aydan."

"I'll make you proud, Momma."

I hugged her close to me. "Winnie, you already make me proud."

Levi came in during our embrace, jumped over the couch, and hugged us both. Winnie giggled as he squeezed.

"Uncle Levi!"

"I wanted a hug too!" he said.

"You are in a good mood," I remarked.

"I am, and we have a date in the morning," he said.

"What?"

"I want to go on a date," Winnie said.

"Sorry, pumpkin. This is just for me and your momma," Levi explained. "I'll take you next time."

"Okay. What's for dinner?" she asked.

"Tacos sounds good," Levi said.

"Tacos," I said.

"Yum. I'm going to see if Bramble and Briar are home," Winnie said and sprinted up the stairs.

"Date?" I asked, turning to Levi.

"Yep," he replied.

"You didn't ask me on a date," I said.

"Grace, will you go on a date with me in the morning?" he asked, then batted his eyelashes. Too ridiculous.

"Sure. Where are we going?" I asked.

"It's a surprise!" he exclaimed. "Let's fix dinner."

"You are going to help?"

"Yep."

"Why are you in such a good mood?"

"I'm going on a date with the most wonderful woman this side of the Otherworld. Why wouldn't I be happy?" He grinned.

"Who is the most wonderful woman on the other side of the Otherworld?"

"I'll let you know."

I slapped him on the shoulder, and we started dinner.

∾

"WE'VE WAITED LONG ENOUGH," I said, as Winnie, Levi, and I stared at our plates.

"Where did they go?" Winnie asked.

"They were out in the woods when I picked you up from Troy's," I said.

"I thought Callum was watching the kids," Levi said.

"Dominick took over at some point during the day, and the boys went outside to play," I said, making light of it.

"*Are they okay?*" Levi asked.

"*Yes, just running from what I can tell. Not afraid,*" I replied.

"Well, these tacos look great," Levi said, taking a bite.

We ate, but we ate in silence. If they were okay, I was going to whip their butts for not coming home in time for dinner. In fact, I'd make them pick their own switch. I'd seen Mrs. Sharolyn do that for one of her grandkids that got out of line. She didn't whip him hard. The humiliation was in having to pick your own method of punishment. Aydan and Callum were too big for whipping, not that I ever would, but I knew that feeling that I'd seen so many moms have over the years when their kids weren't home when they were supposed to be.

Levi cleaned up the dishes, leaving Winnie and me to catch up on some coloring. Bramble and Briar joined us. They were feeling better after their drunken ordeal, but neither of them was sorry for it. In fact, I'd overheard them talking about doing it again. They were going to have to start a Brownies Abominable Anonymous if this kept up.

"They are back," I said quietly as I felt the boys arrive close to the house.

Levi stepped out of the kitchen to wait on them as they came in the door. Winnie put her crayons down and crossed her arms. Their absence had upset her as much as it had me.

They were laughing and joking when they came into the room. Aydan looked at me then at Levi. Callum hung his head and quietly shut the door.

"Mom, we were chasing the Yeti," Aydan said.

"Is that supposed to make me feel better?" I asked.

"I was watching out for him," Callum added.

"Nope. Still don't feel better," I commented.

"Me, either," Winnie said.

"Let me handle this little one," I said, standing up from my position at the coffee table. "Why don't the two of you come have a seat?"

They walked over shyly then sat down on the couch. Levi walked over to where I was, but remained behind me. The motion was clear. He stood behind whatever I had to say to them.

"Mom, I'm sorry," Aydan said.

"I've got a good mind to whip the tar out of both of you, but you are too big for that. However, you have made it very clear that neither of you are grown. No matter what you think you are, neither of you are old enough and experienced enough to be chasing an unknown creature through the woods. What were you going to do when you caught him?" I asked.

They shrugged. "We just wanted to find out more about him," Aydan tried to explain.

"No more. Until this thing with the squirrels and the snow monster is handled, the two of you will stay in this house and do as we say," I said.

"We?" Aydan asked.

"Levi and I," I clarified. "Callum, you are not my child, and I can't make *you* do anything, but I will not have you dragging my son into danger. He may look like a 16-year-old, but he's got a lot to learn about the threats of this world."

"Yes, ma'am," Callum replied.

"We love you both very much. We missed you at dinner, and it wasn't like you not to call or come home," Levi said, softening my harsh tone.

"It won't happen again," Aydan said. "But I am more grown than you think."

"Did you just sass me?" I asked.

"No, ma'am," Aydan replied quickly, realizing his mistake.

I pulled dark and cold power to myself, and the temperature dropped. "Let me be very clear, there is nothing in these woods or in this town that is more dangerous than your mother anxiously waiting for you to come home," I said, then brushed off the power as quickly as I had pulled it in.

Callum and Aydan's eyes were wide with the display.

"There are leftovers in the kitchen. You are probably hungry," Levi said. The boys got up and scampered off to the kitchen.

"*Too much?*" I asked.

"*Nope. My mother used to scare the crap out of me too,*" Levi admitted.

"*Probably not like that,*" I replied.

"*Not exactly the same, but she got her point across,*" Levi said. "*Besides, I love it when you get riled up. It's sexy as hell.*"

"*Get out of here,*" I replied. He grinned before going into the kitchen with the boys. I looked down at Winnie who still seemed mad. "Aydan, come apologize to your sister, too," I said, winking at her. She grinned.

Aydan ran across the room, scooped her up, and hugged her tightly. "I'm sorry, Winnie. I don't want you to worry about me."

"Well, just don't do it again," Winnie said.

Callum joined the hug. "Me too," he said.

"I guess I forgive you," Winnie said.

"Now, back to food," I ordered.

"Yes, ma'am," they replied.

"Thank you, Momma," Winnie said.

"I knew you were just as upset as I was," I said.

"Yeah, but I didn't go all fiery on them," she said.

"This is true," I replied.

"I'll never get in trouble," she said.

"I would like to believe that, but I bet you will," I replied.

"Nope. Elsa is scary," Winnie said.

"Didn't I tell you that I was going to tickle you to death if you called me that again?" I asked.

"Um, no," she said, then took off running across the room. I ran after her until I caught her. We collapsed on the couch as I tickled her without mercy. She shrieked and howled, begging me to stop or for someone to help her. When I finally let her go, she smiled. "I love you, Momma."

"I love you, too. My little wildfire," I said.

CHAPTER SIXTEEN

GRACE SAT CALMLY ON THE COUCH TWIRLING A LONG, BLONDE LOCK *around her finger. Apparently, this part of the story wasn't as painful for her as it was for me. The anticipation of finally being with her was killing me. I knew that we both needed it, but things kept getting in the way. I really thought it was going to be this night after she ripped Callum and Aydan a new one. They deserved it. She worried about them, and she wasn't used to worrying about anyone like that. Even though we both knew they were fine, it was painful to know they didn't think of calling home or checking in with us.*

Our emotions were on edge that night, and I felt the urge to be with her more than ever. But this was the night that changed it all for me. This was the night I realized that I'd become a part of her life for a reason. For me, it was bigger than taking over the Otherworld or ruling in Shady Grove. Maybe it was the inherent love-talker inside of me, but more important than anything else, I realized how big her heart really was. I thought I knew, but I had no idea.

"What are you typing?" she asked.

"Just making some edits," I lied.

"Liar," she said.

I laughed, because she knew me too well. "I'm just adding something important."

"What are you adding?"

"About how frustrated I was during this part of the story."

"I was frustrated, too."

"We both were, but this part was important," I said.

"Yes, it was," she said, breathing a sigh. "We didn't even know how much."

"Go ahead," I urged. She sighed again and continued.

AFTER ALL THE kids were in bed, Levi followed me to my room. We both knew where this was going. The waiting and things interfering with us being together had driven me off the horny block. His footsteps quickened as I reached the bedroom door. He made it to the doorknob before me, then molded his body to mine. As he opened the door, I felt his lips on my neck. Soft kisses while walking us both through the doorway. I hummed as the tingles coursed through my body. I needed more, and so did he.

His fingers curled under the edge of my shirt, tugging it off over my head. I turned around to face him, and he brushed hair out of my face. His hand slid down to my neck, pulling my lips to his.

The dream flashed before my eyes, and I froze in place. He heaved a heavy sigh of frustration.

"I'm sorry," I whispered.

"It's time you told me," he said.

"You are right. It is. Can I tell you after?" I asked, trying to get out of it.

He released me, and backed away. "No."

I watched as he picked up my shirt off the floor, then handed it to me. "I'm not cold," I said.

"No, but your breasts are distracting," he said, as he sat down on the bed. He ran his hands through his hair, then looked at me waiting.

"Right. Well, just remember, I tried to avoid this," I said, putting my shirt back on over my head.

"You've avoided it your whole life, I think," he said.

"Don't get smart with me," I huffed.

"I am not your child, Grace."

"I never said you were. This is painful. This is not a fairy tale. This is *not* a happy ending!"

He held his hand up, offering it to me. I swallowed, and placed my hand in his. He pulled me over to him, and I stood between his legs. His face used my stomach as a pillow.

"Nothing you could ever say to me would change how much I love you. Nothing," he said.

"It will change the way you look at me," I replied.

"Try me," he said, looking up at me with dark navy eyes. I'd never seen them so dark. I was hurting him. Causing him pain. Something I never, ever wanted to do.

"Okay," I whispered, as I climbed up on the bed next to him.

He shifted so that his long legs folded up beneath him. He grabbed my feet and removed my shoes and socks. His hands worked over my feet. I'd never had a fairy rub my feet before. I had lost my train of thought when he brought me back to reality.

"Grace, go ahead," he prompted.

I cleared my throat and tried to decide where to start.

"When I had matured, I found the men in the Otherworld to bore me. Especially in the bedroom. There was no spark. No tingle with any of them. Good sex, yes. But good is such a relative term. I needed more excitement, and not in the kinky ways Bramble and Briar do it."

Levi grinned thinking about the two perverted little brownies.

"Well, I started traveling into the human world. I'd been with a few human men, but saw the effect I had on them."

"I can understand that one," he said.

"Yes, well, it didn't feel right leading them on and not giving them anything in return," I said.

"I'm sure they got something."

"Perhaps, but it wasn't permanent. I didn't understand that need to have someone as your own. Someone to touch your heart. I just wanted the excitement and rush of it."

"And you found it."

"I did. After tiring of the offerings in my father's realm and human men, I hoped to find more. I used my sight to locate men that had a twinge of fairy blood. One day as I shifted from the Otherworld to the human world, I heard the clashing of swords. Normally, I would have shifted right back. The last thing I needed to do was to be in the middle of a war. But this sounded different. Two swords and laughing. I stealthily moved toward the sound of the fight when I found two men who were fully fairy dueling with swords. The longer I watched from my hidden position I realized that the sword one of them carried was none other than Excalibur. The sword of King Arthur. Having read all of Taliesin's stories, I was thrilled to see the Great Sword."

"You didn't know your father was Arthur," Levi said.

"No, I had no idea. What an idiot I was!" I exclaimed.

"No, you weren't. They made a concerted effort to make sure you didn't know," Levi said.

"Yes, well, I watched until the two men finished. One asked the other if he was coming back. The handsome one said that he was going to sit and enjoy the forest before returning to the inn where they were staying. The other man bid him farewell and walked away. He wasn't gone long before the man called out to me."

"I know you are there. Show yourself," the man said.

I stepped out of the bushes where I thought I was hidden to get a better look at him. He, like most fairy men, was built perfectly. His chiseled abs were coated with sweat, and I practically salivated looking at him. I could also tell that he was firmly a winter fairy, as his aura was a bright blue. Under long dark lashes, his eyes were as blue as his aura.

"Hello," I said shyly.

"What are you doing here?" he asked.

"Spying," I replied.

"You should return to your realm. This world is dangerous for your kind," he said.

"Our kind," I corrected him.

He cleaned off the sword with a rag, then stood sheathing it at his side. "No, *your* kind. I do not belong to that world," he said. His tone was harsh, but it didn't sway me.

"I prefer this one myself," I said.

"Are you exiled?" he asked.

"No," I said.

"Then go about your way. You should not even be speaking to me," he replied.

"Wait!" I called out to him before he started to walk away. "Please, wait."

I didn't know why I wanted him so badly, but I did. An exiled fairy was forbidden, but it was the excitement I had wanted. Something taboo. Something dangerous. It thrilled me to think of it.

"You must go. I want nothing to do with you," he said.

"Am I not pleasing to your eye?" I asked.

"No, you're not," he said.

"You're a liar." I laughed.

"My eye may be pleased and even other parts of my body, but I assure you that my heart will not falter."

"Heart! Fairies do not have hearts." His blue eyes flared with anger.

"You are young and unknowing. This world will chew you up and spit you out. Return to the halls of Winter and find your pleasure there," he said, then stalked away.

"After seeing you, there is no pleasure for me there," I replied. He didn't turn when I complimented him. Didn't even flinch.

~

"He rejected you," Levi said.

"Yep. Walked away like I was nothing," I admitted.

"And that turned you on." He smiled.

"It did. It only made it worse than the idea of being with someone I was expressly forbidden to be with." I hung my head in shame.

"Grace, Dylan chose Stephanie before you. Did you go after him because he rejected you?" he asked.

"At first, yes. I wanted to make him regret not waiting for me. But then, he rejected me over and over. So, I returned the favor. We spun around each other like planets around the sun. It was a ridiculous waste of time," I said.

"Because it was just about the sex at first," he said.

"It was. At first. Then, I dunno. I wanted more from him. My heart felt things that it hadn't in a very long time," I said. "Things I swore I'd never feel again."

"Who was he? The man with the sword," Levi asked.

"I cannot say his name. He was forsaken," I said.

"Because of you?"

"Because of us."

"So, eventually, he gave into you."

"Yes."

THE SECOND TIME I saw him he was buying a horse from a man at a stable. I watched him with the animal. It responded to his touch immediately.

"He likes you," I said, before he saw me there.

"I knew I felt a cold draft," he smirked.

"We meet again."

"Only because you have hunted me, and I need to tell you to stop."

"Why?" I asked.

"Because just talking to me will be your death," he said.

"I'm just another fairy. What would my death be to you?"

"If it were because of me, then I would feel it."

"Why? You care nothing for me."

"I never said that. In fact, I think I impressed upon you from the moment I saw you that you needed to go home."

"I don't want to go home. I grow tired of life at court and men who only want position in the King's favor."

"Court? You are high born?"

"I am," I replied. I didn't dare tell him who my father was.

"Are you trained to fight?" he asked. It was common that high born fairy children were taught to fight. I wasn't very good. Mainly because I didn't care enough to learn.

"I have been, but I admit that I'm not very good."

"You are not good, because you don't care." It was weird that he could read me so well.

"Then teach me," I replied.

He stared at me for a moment. "Meet me in the woods tomorrow at the same spot. Bring your weapon. If you best me, then I will give you what you want."

I swayed my hips walking up to him. He was unmovable. I saw the flicker of desire, but a resolution in him to not touch me. So, I touched him. I ran my finger down his arm. The tingle shot through me, but he didn't respond.

"I bet you cannot fathom what I want," I said.

He stepped a half-step closer to me, looking down into my eyes. "I bet that I can fathom a lot, Vixen. I assure you that you have nothing that I haven't already sampled."

"Perhaps," I said, then left him with his horse.

"Vixen. That actually works," Levi said.

"Shut-up. It does not," I said.

"It doesn't now, but I bet it did then. You laid it on thick. I've seen it."

I remembered the night I tried to seduce Levi, and he withstood it. Easily. He may have trembled at my touch, but he turned the tables on me.

"I'm sorry about that night, Levi. I was wrong to do that," I said.

He touched my cheek, and I leaned into his hand. "Grace, that seems like ages ago. We are so far past that, although I kicked myself for not giving in."

I laughed at him. "You did not."

"I did. I'm not as righteous as you would like to think. You know what I am capable of with this guitar. I could make any woman do exactly what I wanted them to do, then they would beg me for more," he said. If I didn't know Levi better, I would have thought he was bragging, but I knew that he wasn't. Well, maybe a little.

"I think you are a good man because you have that power, yet you don't use it. Even now with me, you don't," I said.

"I'm not in the business of forcing women to do things against their will," Levi said. "And I'll gut any man that does."

"Nope. You aren't righteous at all." I smiled.

"Did you meet him the next day?" He changed the subject back to the story.

"I did."

I WAITED for almost an hour in the clearing where I had first saw him. When he arrived, he seemed upset.

"I cannot do this today. I must go," he said.

"What's wrong?" I asked.

"My friend who was here with me is sick. I must return to him," he said.

"You can't heal him?" I asked.

"No, I'm not sure what ails him."

"He is fairy."

"Yes, which is why I must go. He should not be sick," he said.

"A curse?" I asked.

"Maybe," he said.

"I can go with you," I offered.

"No! I told you. This is a bad idea."

"But here you are," I said.

"My lady. I am nothing to pursue. You have some notion in your head that this is exciting or thrilling, but it's real life. Go home. Do not return here."

"You keep the Great Sword. You cannot be nothing."

He moved faster than I expected, and before I realized, he had me backed against the tree with his thumb pressed into my neck.

"How do you know about the sword?"

"I've read the stories," I said.

"Fairies don't read," he growled.

"I do. I love Taliesin's stories."

He pressed harder. "Who did you tell about the sword?"

"No one," I gasped as he pressed. "Please. You are hurting me."

He released me and stepped back. "You did not lie."

"Fairies cannot lie."

"No, but you can be manipulative."

"I spoke the truth. I've told no one there about you or the sword."

"Have you come to take it from me? Is that what this is? You plan to seduce me, then take the sword?"

"No. I don't want the sword."

"Leave. Do not come back here."

I felt nothing from him. Not even a tingle or a spark. "I'm sorry."

I wasn't sure why I apologized, but I ran off into the forest to find the nearest tree to shift home. When I did, Finley was waiting on me.

"Whatever you are doing is going to get you in trouble," Finley said.

"It doesn't matter. I'm not going back," I said.

"Who is he?"

"I don't know. Some asshole who rejects me. He is angry and hurt," I said.

"I've never known you to choose a charity case, Glory."

"It's not a charity case. He's fuckable. That's it."

"Then, you can stop going back."

"I'm not going back. I've already said that, Fin. Go be an asshole to someone else. I've had enough fairy asshole today," I said.

"He's fairy?"

"No. He's not," I said, but the lie hung between us. Finley knew the answer was false.

His tone changed, dripping with pity. "Glory. Cavorting with an exiled fairy will get you banished. Please don't go back. What would I do if I lost you?"

"I'm not going back," I said. I meant it, but as the days passed, I wondered what happened to his friend. Perhaps I could have helped. I knew that I had to go back. Even if it was just to help his friend. He didn't seem to have many, so I needed to try.

I snuck into my father's room and took his mirror. If you looked through it, a curse, malady, or ailment could be revealed. Then, when there was a huge celebration in the castle, I slipped out unnoticed.

When I reached the town closest to the spot in the forest, it only took a couple of inquiries to locate the man. He was still sick, and his friend had gone to look for help. I found his friend near death. Pulling out the mirror, I looked into it. Long tendrils of power leeched on his body draining him of life. It was a curse. A fairy witch's curse.

Back then I knew more about magic because it was a daily exercise. I waved my hand over his body, drawing the curse to me. It wrapped around my hand as it released from his body. His shallow breathing became deeper. I heard footsteps approaching, and I knew his friend was returning. The power dropped the temperature in the room, and the windows iced up.

His friend burst into the room, "What are you doing?"

I looked from the curse to him, and in doing so, lost control over it. It began to sink back on to the man. "Help me," I said to him.

"What do I do?"

"I need more power," I said, feeling that he had charged himself to perform the spell. His hand slid down my arm. Tingles raced through my body as his power met mine. The curse responded, lifting off of the man. "I know how to remove it, but I don't know what to do with it."

He reached into his pocket with his free hand and opened a small vial of blue water. He poured it over our linked arms and the curse dissipated. I jerked away from him, shaking the power from my hands frantically. He stooped over his friend to check his breathing, then turned back to me. By this time, my whole body was shaking.

Drawing me into his arms, he pressed me to his body. "That was a stupid thing to do, my Lady."

"You should have let me help," I stammered.

"You shouldn't be involved," he said. His tone with me had changed. It sounded regretful more than anything. "Thank you."

"You are welcome," I replied. His lips lightly touched my cheek, and I almost fainted with the surge of attraction. That tingle. He kept me upright, but I knew then, he felt it too.

"You should go," he said.

"I'm not going," I replied.

"What is your name?" he asked.

"Glory," I replied.

"That's beautiful. Very fitting," he said.

"Who are you?"

"My friends call me Cohen," he said.

"Do not send me away," I begged.

"I will meet you tomorrow in the forest as promised before to teach you," he said.

I sighed in disappointment, because once again he was rejecting me.

∿

LEVI LOOKED AT ME STRANGELY. "Who was his friend? What was his name?"

"I don't know. He never told me. He said that his friend had fallen in love with someone that he shouldn't have, and that someone else cursed him. A love triangle. I guess it had finally caught up to him," I shrugged.

Levi bounded off the bed and crossed the room to lean forward on the window sill.

"It was Jeremiah," he said.

"No, it wasn't," I denied it.

"It was. He told me when he brought me here, that he owed you for saving his life once. He said he was at death's door, and that you came along for no reason other than love, to heal him. He said you restored his life. He said that he wanted to find a way to make it up to you. I think he felt like bringing you to Shady Grove was his redemption," Levi explained.

"I never healed Jeremiah. Not to mention all the bad things and lies that he told once he brought me here. Erasing my memories. I hardly call that redemption," I said.

"He was fighting on three battlegrounds. As a Sanhedrin, he had a doctrine to follow. As a servant of your father, he had another. Then he had his own loyalties to Riley, and we know that loyalty to your children supersedes everything. I think he erased your memories because he was trying to keep you in Shady Grove. Keep you in the middle of this world, so that one day, you could do what you are doing now. Lead these people which includes his daughter," he said.

"It wasn't Jeremiah," I protested.

"You didn't realize it was him, Grace. I bet his glamour was much younger. You said he was fairy through your sight. Was he green or blue?"

"Green."

He crossed back to me. "Your lover's best friend was Jeremiah Freyman. Tristan, a knight of the round table. So, who was the man you fell in love with?" Levi asked. He reached up and touched my cheek. "Grace, you've always had more heart that you wanted to admit. You have to realize that all of this goes back to this man. Whoever he was."

"He was the heir to Arthur's throne. He was given the sword by the Lady of the Lake after Belvedere threw it back. I did not know it then that my father's hatred of him was based on the legends. I didn't know my father was the legend, so when Astor told me everything in Summer, it hit me like a ton of bricks. And Finley knew! Everyone knew except me. And…" I stopped mid-rant because I could not say his name. No matter how many times I tried to form it on my lips, I couldn't. He was forsaken. He died because he loved me. I looked back up to Levi who had gone pale as if he'd seen a ghost. "Levi?"

" I'm fine. It's just overwhelming," he said.

"Do you know who I am talking about?" I asked.

"No. I'll look it up in the books, but not now. Finish the story," he urged.

"It's not a happy ending," I said.

"I know, but we both need to hear you tell it," he said.

Fucking bard. I had gotten to the point where I didn't want to hurt anymore. Dylan's death was a renewal of the death of the man I called Cohen.

I ARRIVED at the meeting place only to be astounded once again by this man. He arrived in the cloak of a priest. I watched him remove the cloak, revealing his common breeches and tunic underneath.

"What should I call you?" I asked staring at the vestments.

"I took orders many years ago. I am no longer in the faith," he said.

"I didn't say anything about the cloak."

"I know, but your gaze is fixed upon it."

"Perhaps. So, what shall I call you?"

"Whatever you wish to call me, Glory."

For every time that my brother called me Glory, I cringed. But when it rolled off his lips, it was like he was meant to say my name. I wanted to hear him say it, preferably during a sexual climax. But once again, it didn't seem like we were headed in that direction.

"What do you go by?" I asked.

"Cohen," he replied.

"Fine, Cohen," I repeated.

"Show me what you can do," he said.

I raised my small sword against the Great One. It hummed in his hands, and the vibration of the blade grew louder when it neared me. After a couple of simple parries, he looked at the sword then at me.

"It knows you," he said.

"What?"

"The sword knows you. It knows your blood," he said. "Who are you, Glory?"

"Just a fairy," I replied.

He wrinkled his forehead knowing it wasn't a lie, but an omission. He came at me harder. I fought off the blows, but had no chance of any offensive strikes against him.

"You should be better than this if you were trained," he said.

"I wasn't a good student," I replied.

He grunted, then looked back at Excalibur. "Part of your problem is that you do not have a proper weapon. The sword you have cannot match this one. However, I have an idea. Meet me here tomorrow, and we will try something different."

He placed his sword in its sheath and donned his cloak.

"That's it?" I asked.

"Yes, we will pick up your lessons tomorrow," he said.

"Cohen, I don't want to sword fight with you," I huffed.

"Ah! There is the spoiled brat I expected to see." He laughed.

"I'm not coming back," I said.

He mounted his horse, smiling down at me. "Yes, you are."

Then rode off leaving me holding my sword and covered in sweat. Not the good kind of sweat either.

He was right. I couldn't resist, being in his presence or getting the chance to know him more. I had to return. When I did, I found him waiting for me with two curved short swords or daggers. The hilts were leather bound and tied tightly. No adornments. Nothing fancy.

"Here, this will work better with your smaller frame, your speed, and give you another hand. One to defend, one to strike. You have no shield, so you must defend yourself with the blade," he instructed without a hello or greeting.

"Nice to see you too, Cohen. Thank you for asking. I had a wonderful day," I said.

He grinned. "Good afternoon, Glory. Now, give them a try." He handed me the blades and I took them. I had to admit I liked the way they felt in my hands much more than the sword I had been using. He showed me how to handle them and as the sun set, he suggested we try one round with them versus Excalibur.

He started with his stance prepared for me to strike first. He was giving me the opportunity to do more than just defend myself. I used my dominant hand to shield myself from his sword and stepped to strike him with the other hand. He dodged it, clanging his weapon against the one in my right hand.

"You get the idea, but you can't go for the kill to start off. You need to learn your opponent," he said.

"I know my opponent."

"Do you?"

"I do. He carries the Great Sword. He wears a priest's cloak and acts like he's as celibate as one, despite his insistence that he isn't of the faith anymore."

"You don't know me at all, Glory."

He stepped forward to strike, and I defended again with my right hand.

"Tell me where I am wrong."

"You have been nothing but wrong since we met."

I huffed as we traded a few more blows. He was toying with me.

"Shut up and fight!" I yelled at him.

He turned it up a notch, and I found myself defending again with both weapons. It was hopeless. I was never going to beat him, and he certainly wasn't going to give in to me. This was a game, and I had tired of it.

I stepped out of the exchange, causing him to stumble.

"What's wrong?"

"I'm tired of you toying with me."

"I'm not playing a game," he insisted.

"Yes, you are. Thank you for these, but you keep them," I said handing him back the small swords.

"I had them made for you."

"I don't want them. Take them back," I said.

He looked to the swords, then back to me. "What do you want from me, Glory? Just a fuck and move on? It seems to me that you could have any man on earth or below it. Why me? I'm the one person that could cost you your life."

"It's not about that anymore. It's about the fact that I've done everything you have asked me, plus I helped your friend, and yet, you show me no regard. Nothing. I feel like an idiot thinking you were different. That *this* might be something worth fighting for. Father was right. Our lives are not fairy tales. I was a fool for thinking I might find a small piece of one!" I yelled.

Anger filled his face, and he launched himself toward me at a pace that I couldn't match as I backed up. Eventually, I backed into a tree where he pinned me with his arms on each side of my body. I dropped the swords to the ground.

His voice deepened as he tried to control his fury. "Your father is right. Fairy tales are things that humans tell, because they need to escape the harsh reality that this world is nothing but a distance between birth and death. Even for us. It's just a matter of time."

"Don't you want more?" I whimpered.

"What? So, I can be like my friend? So, I can lose my heart to a woman only to find myself cursed? No, thank you. Go home to your Daddy, Glory," he said.

"Let her go," Finley said behind him. I hadn't seen Finley appear, but he must have been following me again.

Cohen spun around lifting the Great Sword. It hummed louder as he approached Finley who didn't flinch or back down.

"Please, stop. He's my brother," I pleaded. "Cohen, please."

"A white-haired fairy. Two white-haired fairies. Do you know how rare that is?" Cohen asked, holding the sword up.

"Very," Finley said. "Glory, go home. I'll handle this."

"There is nothing to handle. We had a misunderstanding," I said.

"He's trying to scare you away, and you are just stubborn enough not to buy it. Go home, Gloriana."

Cohen lowered the sword. I couldn't see his face, but I heard it in his voice. Finley had given me away.

"Gloriana."

"Yes," I replied.

"Daughter of Oberon. Heir to the Winter throne?"

"Yes."

"I am cursed already," he said, sinking to his knees. I ran to him, falling to the ground before him.

"I didn't tell you because I don't tell anyone. I didn't want you to look at me differently," I said.

He lifted his hand to my cheek, then slid it down behind my neck. "Glory, he will kill us both for this."

"We haven't *done* anything," I protested.

"That's great. You should get up and come with me," Finley said. He walked over to me, offering me his hand to stand up.

"Go with him and forget that we ever met," Cohen said.

"I can't. You are a part of me now," I said. "That won't go away."

He pulled me closer. I had waited for so long for him to touch me, and now it only caused him pain. "This is a long rivalry. So many years of misunderstanding. He will not let this go. I am already dead."

"What? I don't understand," I said. "Is it because he wants the sword?"

Cohen lifted his eyes to Finley, asking a question that he did not voice.

"She does not know," Finley said.

"Why?" Cohen asked.

"It keeps her safe," Finley said.

"Know what?" I insisted.

"Our father has many enemies. Some of his own making. Cohen here, is one of those enemies. But watching him with you, I am sure that it is some sort of mistake," Finley said. "But you should still go home, Glory. Too much is at stake."

"You both are treating me like a child. Does what I want matter?" I asked.

"No," they answered.

"Please, I'd rather stay with you than to ever go back to the Otherworld," I said to Cohen, ignoring my brother's insistence.

"Glory, you deserve more than what I can give you. You do have a heart in there somewhere. You will find the right person to give it to, and he will be damn lucky. It's not me," he said.

"I'm not leaving," I stated.

"Yes, you are," Finley said.

"Shut up, Fin," I snapped, then threw myself at Cohen. I landed in his arms and pressed against his body. I took the momentary shock to kiss him.

Magic fired between us as our lips connected. The overwhelming attraction broke through his wall as he joined in the kiss. Deeper and deeper I fell with each motion. His rigid body relaxed accepting mine to his.

Finley backed away quietly, knowing he had lost his efforts to save me from disaster.

I broke from Cohen's lips breathing hard. Looking into his eyes, I asked him, "You know my name. It's only fair that I know yours."

He told me his name, and I knew exactly who he was. I didn't understand how or why he was still alive after his reign, but he was here. And in his arms was the only place I wanted to be.

"Glory, do you understand what a huge mistake you've made?" he asked, as he undressed me.

"Yes, and I care not. I just want you. I want to feel more," I begged.

~

"I DON'T NEED to know the details," Levi said, staring down at his hands.

"I wasn't going to tell you," I replied. "But it did happen then."

"He made you tingle like me," he said with a lowered voice.

I moved closer to him on the bed, forcing his chin up to look at me. "No."

"No?"

"It's so much stronger with you. I knew that the day you kissed me at the Food Mart. It blew me away," I said.

"Why?"

"Why is it that way?" I asked. He nodded. "Hell, I don't know, Levi. I can't tell you why. But my heart already belonged to Dylan."

"I knew that," he said.

"What is left of it is yours."

"I want it all," he said.

Once again, the tingle of our attraction rippled over me as his hand found my neck. It must have been a love talker signature move. Memory and reality mixed as he kissed my neck. I moved closer, inviting him to do more. Levi's lips were soft, but his hands were rough. The combination was perfect. I couldn't understand how this man who matured so quickly had become everything that I desired.

Then the scratching above our heads began.

"Ignore it," he grumbled.

"Okay," I said, laying back on the bed. Levi climbed over me as the noise intensified.

"Bramble! Get the squirrel in the attic!" Levi shouted, startling me.

"Levi!"

"No, Grace. Not this time!"

I giggled as the sounds of footsteps joined the scratching.

"Um, that's more than one squirrel," I said.

Levi shifted his hips to remind me of why we were here. I bit my lip while he hovered over me.

"It's just a couple of squirrels," he said, as the ceiling opened up and squirrels poured into my bedroom from the attic.

I screamed and darted off the bed.

"NO!" Levi yelled as he swatted them off the bed. They scampered around the room, chewing on furniture, climbing through the drawers of my bureau, and darting into the bathroom.

"I'm going to get the kids," I said, running for the door.

"I'm going to kill them all!" Levi said, flinging one across the room with a swat. It bounced off the wall and kept going. "Indestructible squirrels! Really?!"

"Rufus! Get 'em boy!" I called out to my dachshund.

Rufus started yipping as he ran up the steps. Several of them darted out of the bedroom, and the short-legged dog stopped to let out an angry growl. His barks filled the house as he started chasing them around the rooms.

CHAPTER SEVENTEEN

CHAOS. PURE UTTER CHAOS. WINNIE RAN OUT OF HER ROOM followed by Bramble and Briar who were swooping down at the bushy-tailed invaders.

"Summon the army, my Love!" Bramble yelled.

"Yes, Sir!" Briar snapped. She revealed a small horn and began tooting on it loudly.

Aydan came out of his room sans shirt scratching his head. "What is going on?"

"Get a shirt on. We are being invaded!" I screamed. He looked down at his feet where the squirrels scampered.

"I've got this," he said, shifting to a bird. His large wings filled the hallway as he went after the grey creatures. They dashed behind furniture. I ran down the hall, scooping up a screaming Winnie on the way. I met Callum going up the stairs as I ran down.

"What the hell?" he said.

"I'm taking Winnie to the truck. Open the doors. Let them out!" I said. He changed direction to open the door for us as I rushed out with Winnie in my arms. We ran to the truck where I tossed her in quickly and jumped in the truck. *"We are going to Hot Tin."*

"I'll meet you there," Levi said. I could hear the disappointment

and frustration in his voice. This whole debacle was getting pretty ridiculous. Even for Shady Grove standards.

Winnie whimpered as we drove to Nestor's place. "I'm sorry, honey. I had no idea there were so many in the house."

"Why are they in the house?" she asked.

"It seems like someone has decided to put a curse on us that is rather annoying," I said.

"Why?"

I slowed the truck. "Winnie, there are people and fairies in this world that do not like me and the people living in Shady Grove. Sometimes they do mean things to us, but we fight through it."

"Like when Mrs. Robin put Daddy in a jar," she said.

"Yes, like that," I said.

"Are you going to kill her?" she asked.

No sense in hiding it from her. "Yes, I am."

"Good."

HOT TIN WAS QUIET, thankfully. No massive attack of squirrels. Nestor took Winnie upstairs into his apartment to let her watch television. I called across town to my knights who all were experiencing similar attacks.

"Squirrels! Of all things!" I huffed.

"They are easily controlled," a voice said behind me.

I turned around to see a man covered in hair matted with snow. His facial features were hardened, but his ice blue eyes were kind.

"You!" I exclaimed. "You are just as bad. My sons chased you through the forest."

He chuckled and snow fell from his hairy body. Thankfully he wore a pair of leather shorts across his manhood. I like all different kinds of men, but I wasn't into hairy ones.

"*Levi. Yeti. Hot Tin. Now.*"

Levi appeared beside me, holding Excalibur. I touched the blade of the sword, pushing it down.

"Ah! Bard! I love music. We should play together," he said.

"Yeah, sure. The Bard and Yeti Band," I quipped.

"The yeti has a long tradition of music much like a bard's magic," he said.

"Well, that's great. Why are you in Shady Grove?" Levi asked.

"Snow. I don't find it in this region often," he said.

"I did that," I admitted.

"I see, Fairy Queen," he said with a reverent nod.

"Is that your only business here?" I asked.

"Yes, that's all. I've met a few of your servants," he said.

"You got my brownies drunk," I said.

"I make a powerful brew. You should try it. I promise that it will not have the same effect on you. It's magic effects the weak-minded which neither of you are. In fact, I'm quite impressed with the dynamic here. A town full of dark fairies prone to mischievous and dark behavior, yet they work together under your rule," he said.

"Thank you. I think. Do you intend to stay here?" I asked.

"Perhaps. I seem to be misplaced from my own region," he said.

"Where are you from?" I asked.

"Tibet. I was captured by supernatural hunters and brought here on a ship. I managed to get away from them at a port. I followed my instincts here to the snow," he explained.

"A port? Did you land in Steelshore?" Levi asked.

"Indeed. That is the name of the city," he said.

"Importing supernaturals?" Levi asked.

"Focus. We have enough trouble here with the squirrels," I said.

"I saw the annoying little critters, then your brownies told me about them. Perhaps I can help," he said.

"Do you have a name?" I asked.

"I am called Tashi," he replied.

"Nice to meet you, Tashi," I said, offering my hand to him.

His hair-covered palm grasped mine. I felt the deep cold inside of him. A cold magic. It felt familiar like my own dark power. He noticed it too, raising a snowy eyebrow.

"What do you suggest for the squirrels?" Levi asked.

"I'm pretty sure that if we can get them all a little of my micro-brew, I can persuade them to follow me out of town," he explained.

"Like a pied piper?" I asked.

"Exactly like it," he smiled.

I nudged Levi. "You probably could have done that."

"I've been distracted," Levi muttered.

I giggled, because unfortunately, we were still distracted. "You owe me a date," I said.

He smiled and released his tension. "Yes, I do. I forgot about that. It was kind of a long night," he said.

"Yeah," I replied.

The door of Hot Tin swung open, and Mike, the vape guy, stepped inside. "Ah! I see you have met Tashi."

"We have. How do you know him?" I asked.

"He just came by the shop looking for some rare ingredients for his brew. It just so happened that I had exactly what he needed," Mike explained.

"I might need more, Mike. We are going to use the brew on the squirrels," Tashi explained.

"Brilliant idea!" Mike exclaimed. "I'll go gather up everything I have. Come with me and we can use my lab to make it."

"I have to make it in my backpack," Tashi said with a bang on the metal pack.

"Well, come on, we have work to do," Mike said. "Levi, we will let you know when we are ready."

Mike left with the Yeti as Nestor fielded calls about the squirrel plague. He instructed everyone to come down to Hot Tin. We'd pack everyone in and explain the plan to them. I was sure everyone needed a drink. I knew I did. The horny fairy inside of me needed to chill out.

"Mind if I fix a drink?" Levi asked Nestor.

He held his hand over the receiver of his old corded phone. "Of course not. Help yourself. Fix Grace one too. She needs it."

I grinned, because Nestor probably knew intuitively exactly what was bothering us. Levi poured whiskey in two glasses, then added a couple of pieces of ice. He held one up for me. I took it and we clinked glasses. He chugged his all at once.

"That bad?" I asked.

"Yes," he grumbled. "And you aren't finished with the story."

"The rest is just banishment and death," I said.

"I think I need to know," he said, refilling his glass.

"As soon as this is over," I said.

"I'm tired of waiting for everything. Tired of Brockton and his minions causing us problems. Tired of Stephanie and the witches along with Rhiannon. I'm tired of waiting for you!" he fussed.

"Pitch a hissy fit, then," I said with a smile.

"Don't make fun of me, Grace," he mumbled.

"Levi, I feel exactly the same but we can't rush the takeover of Winter. I think we will only get one shot at it. We can't mess it up. As for me and you, I love you, Levi. Nothing is going to stop us from the path we are on. We might be delayed, but it's not going to stop us from being together," I said.

He sat his glass down and placed his hand over mine. I turned mine upward to grasp his. That thrum between us was still there. It would always be there. I hadn't lied. Levi's effect on me was far deeper than Cohen's. I didn't know why it was so different or so much more intense, but it was. In fact, out of all it, Levi's revelation that Jeremiah was Cohen's friend shook me.

Jeremiah brought Levi to me as if he knew exactly what I would need. Dylan was already here, and Jeremiah knew how I felt about him because of all the times that he erased my memory. Yet, he brought Levi anyway. And my father had given Taliesin's gift to Levi. He knew too.

"What is it?" Levi asked.

"Jeremiah, you, my father. I'm just trying to understand," I said.

Nestor had been listening and hung up the phone. "I can give you some insight to it."

"You can?" I asked.

"Yes, because Jeremiah was in charge of all of us here. Our keeper. But he also worked for your father. Rhiannon is the one who decides who lives here, and that was carried out by Jeremiah. He was bound to her because of Riley. I didn't know Riley was his daughter, but I knew she had something on him. I never asked him what possessed him to mate with the Queen of Summer, but I wish

I had. But back to you and Levi and Dylan. Dylan was brought here for you. He came here for you, but the moment he stepped into town, he chose Stephanie without even seeing you. The night you walked in here, and he was leaving with her. I saw the two of you look at each other. I also saw that twinge of regret immediately with him. Jeremiah told me that your father had prepared someone for you, but that he wasn't ready because his mother was sick."

"Me," Levi said.

"Yes, so Jeremiah brought Dylan here, but he ordered Jeremiah to bring Levi here," Nestor said. "Dylan knew why Levi was here. Jeremiah in anger had told him he was being replaced which is why I think he finally ran off Stephanie, so that he could at least try with you."

"I miss him," I said quietly. Levi squeezed my hand.

"We all do," Nestor said. "He made everything right in the end. I suspect he helped Levi here see how important he was to you while they were in the Otherworld."

"He did," Levi said. "A story that I need to tell."

"I'm not sure I'm ready for it," I said. "No matter how many times I wonder what happened down there, I just think I'm not ready."

"Whenever you are, I'll tell you everything," Levi said.

"You should tell him about *him*," Nestor said.

"Cohen. I have started. He knows how we met and that my father wanted him dead," I said.

"Most of us in town know that story, Grace. I know you probably didn't realize it, but it makes you even more one of us. There are many of us here that chose love over a safe place in the Otherworld. I chose it for the love of my daughter. Luther chose it for Betty. Eugene for Chaz. Amanda for Troy. Dylan for you," he said. "Levi for you."

"There are more. Tennyson came here for Jenny. Astor came here for you, but found Ella. Finley came here for you. I imagine that Ford came here because Wendy wanted to be here. Joey is back here for his son, Devin. My father came here for me. Dominick came here for a family. It's always been about choosing danger for the ones we love," Levi said. "That will bind us together to win. You are that example."

A tear rolled down my cheek. I suppose it was time to admit that I had always had a heart. I shut it off after Cohen died. Little by little people came into my life to remind me it was there. Miss Sharolyn. The trailer park girls that coaxed me into getting a tattoo. Remy. Jeremiah. Winnie. And when Dylan came along it awakened, and I remembered the boldness of love. We needed that boldness going forward, and I had it inside of me. I just needed to share it with everyone in Shady Grove.

Levi's frustration evaporated, as he watched me mull over these things. He smiled and his deep blue eyes resembled the night sky with a light reflecting in them like a star.

"You barded me again," I said.

"I have not yet begun to bard you." He grinned, then placed a soft kiss on my forehead.

≈

WE WERE JOINED by representatives from every race in town at the bar. Squeezing into the small space, we were packed in like sardines. Levi stood on a chair so that everyone could see him.

"Tashi, the yeti, has agreed to help us with the squirrels," he announced. The crowd murmured with disbelief. Levi explained the plan and once again asked for everyone to be patient.

"Who is doing it?" someone asked that I couldn't see.

"We aren't sure. Our goal is to get rid of them and find out what we can about that as we go," Levi said.

"It's a curse!" Mrs. Frist yelled. It stirred up the crowd. I jumped up on the chair that Levi was standing in. He grabbed my waist to steady me on the edge of the chair. I was glad it didn't collapse.

"Maybe it is, but that doesn't mean that it will stop us. Hell, we are all cursed. If whoever it is wants to throw a plague of squirrels at us, then so be it. We will push through this like everything else. If this is the best they've got, then I laugh at their efforts. My brownies have more bravery than some of you. Time to buck up and put your big girl panties on. There is a fight coming and if you let a few squirrels stop you, then we are all doomed. It is going to take all of us to take back the Otherworld," I said.

"What if we don't care about the fight?" Mrs. Frist asked.

"Then you can get your ass out of my town," I said.

"*Grace*," Levi chided.

I cleared my throat. "Actually, no. You can stay, but we will always know what a coward you are. Everyone is welcome to stay, but when this is over, you will have to look at yourself in the mirror and live with your decision. Because I promise you, I won't care. Ain't nobody got time for that." A ripple of laughter crossed the room, and I knew the majority of them were with us.

"So, as soon as the brew is ready, we will tempt the squirrels with it, and allow our yeti friend to lead them out of town," Levi said. "In the meantime, stay safe and take whatever precautions you need to take for your families."

The meeting broke up, and the citizens of Shady Grove moved into the parking lot around Hot Tin. Some stayed inside, and I helped Nestor serve drinks while Levi went to check on Tashi and Mike's progress. The sooner we got these damn squirrels out of town, the sooner I could give my bard exactly what he needed. And get a little for myself. I smiled with the thought of it. Nestor nudged me.

"I had my doubts about Levi, but I see that look. I know what that means," Nestor said.

"It means that I've been a very fortunate woman to find more than one man that can make me completely happy," I said.

"Extremely fortunate," he said. "Fortune has smiled on you, but some things are fated."

"Fated. Really? I didn't take you for that kind of romantic."

"I am when I see it happening to someone I love."

He meant me. I grinned and hugged him tightly. "I love you, Grandfather." He squeezed me back because I rarely called him by that name. He'd always been Nestor to me, and I didn't feel the need to change it, but perhaps it wasn't about what I needed and more about what he needed. From now on, I vowed to call him as he deserved to be called.

I checked on Winnie, and she had fallen asleep in the center of a pile of crayons and artwork. Before I could get to her, Levi appeared. He lifted her up and nodded for me to come closer. I placed my hand on the strings of his guitar.

"Home."

CHAPTER EIGHTEEN

FINISHING THE STORY WASN'T ON MY MIND, BUT IT WAS DEFINITELY on his. His demeanor had changed, but I couldn't tell what was different. We couldn't go upstairs because the bed was covered in sheetrock and dust.

"Why are you insisting on this now?" I asked.

"I need to know," he said.

"Levi."

"Grace."

I huffed and sat down on the couch. Thankfully, we decided to finish this in the living room instead of the bedroom. I had half a mind to make him wait a little bit longer, but my fairy protested. Levi sat on the chair across from me with attentive blue eyes.

"Fine."

AFTER COHEN and I were together, I didn't go back home. It wasn't long before my father came looking for me. We managed to hide through the use of distractions, cantrip spells, and wards. Eventually, Oberon caught up with us.

Cohen and I had been living in an Inn where the owner had access to a druid. The druid helped us set up some protection spells, and one day he showed up with a witch who added to those spells.

It didn't matter. My father walked right through all of them. His clothes were singed, but he was unscathed.

Cohen stepped in front of me as my father entered the room with his guards. A large contingent of harpies who could barely contain their glamours. My brother stood with them. I saw the pain in his eyes. He hadn't told on us, but father knew that he had kept our secret.

"My King," Cohen said, dipping his head.

"I was never your king," Oberon replied bitterly.

"But you were for a time before you passed into the world below," Cohen said with reverence.

"Speak not of those things," my father warned with his eyes on me. I didn't dare ask what they meant. My father's gaze intimidated me. I feared his wrath. Mostly for Cohen. I had forced this relationship. I would never regret it. Or so I thought.

"Gloriana, you will return home. The council has discovered your affair with this exile. You will be punished, and there is nothing I can do to stop it. If you don't return, you will disgrace me more than you already have," Father said.

"Your Majesty, I give you my life in place of hers," Cohen said.

"No!" I exclaimed.

"At least you do have an honorable bone in your body, however, you too shall face judgment," Oberon said. "You can come willingly or my guards will take you."

Cohen spun around to me, placing his hands on my cheeks. He looked deep into my eyes as if he were looking inside of me. "When they ask you, you tell them I compelled you."

"No," I grunted, trying to jerk away from him.

He held my face in place, looking into my soul. "When they ask you, you tell them, I compelled you to love me. I compelled you to stay. Say it, Gloriana."

I tried holding it back, but the power of his influence was too great. He was compelling me to lie. He'd never forced me to do anything until this point. I snarled.

"Say it, Glory!"

"You compelled me to love you. You compelled me to stay," I repeated, as tears rolled down my cheeks.

His lips captured mine, and I got lost in the connection one last time. Gasping for air when he finished. "I love you, Gloriana."

"And, I you."

He released me and willingly walked out with the harpies, leaving me alone with my father and Finley.

"Daughter, I warned you about these activities. The human world is not a place for a Queen. You will have to give up your lands inside of winter. You will be a Queen no more. I will lose you," he grunted. "All for a love-talking fool."

"Fin," I cried.

"Glory, they are going to exile you," Finley said. "You will not be family to us anymore."

"What about him?" I choked on the words.

"He will be forsaken," my father growled as he swept out of the room.

"No," I cried. "Please, no." Finley helped me to my feet, and I walked mindlessly to the first tree in sight. He opened the way and I stepped through to my doom.

"I DON'T KNOW why I didn't consider Finley's part in all of this," Levi said.

"He was there. He warned me, and I didn't listen," I said.

"You never considered that perhaps he ratted you out?"

"He didn't," I insisted.

"How do you know?" he asked.

"Because Father punished him too."

"Damn," Levi said. "Keep going."

"I really don't want to," I said. He didn't budge.

~

My "TRIAL" ended quickly with an edict to exile me from the Otherworld. However, instead of escorting me out of the kingdom, I was forced to watch Cohen's verdict.

When they asked me if he had compelled me to love him, his magic stirred inside of me and I spoke the words he'd given me. Nothing could hold them back. I hated myself for it.

They sat me in a chair facing Cohen. He knelt on the cold, stone floor of the court. His head was bowed with his hair hanging down around his face. He would not look up to me. My father and brother were behind me along with several of his court and knights.

"The council has found that this man willfully and deceptively took the daughter of the King to his bed against her will. He knew that even speaking to her could cost him his life. Let his name be stricken from all accounts and every tongue in the Kingdom will forget him," one of the councilmen said.

"Let it be so," my father concurred.

"I move that Oberon's daughter, Gloriana, face the same destiny. She has wronged, not only her father, but she has slighted Summer as well," a female voice said.

"My Queen, you are here to observe. You will not speak my daughter's name again. Are we clear?" Oberon said. I couldn't see who he was speaking to. A queen could be any female with royal blood who was the overseer of lands in Winter. I had lands there that belonged to me. I was their ruler, making me a Queen. However, I was sure that it was Rhiannon, Queen of Summer.

The female did not respond verbally to my father.

"Carry on," Oberon instructed.

"His life is now forfeit. He shall never walk the earth above or the world below. Shall we commence the execution?"

"Yes," my father said.

"No!" I screamed, then I felt a wave of magic flow over me. Cold to its core. Dark and lonely. My mouth closed by force, and I could not speak.

A hooded man approached Cohen, then grabbed a handful of his hair, jerking his head backwards. I could see his blue eyes then, looking upward to the ceiling. The hooded man drew a long dagger and swept it quickly across his throat. The blood poured freely from the wound. His head slumped, and his eyes finally met mine. He smiled, then died.

His body fell over in the pool of blood.

"Bring me the sword," Father said.

The man who announced the sentence walked past me holding Excalibur up. I heard him kneel behind me to offer the sword to my father. I took that moment as my chance. I darted across the stone floor to Cohen's body. Rolling him over, I realized that he was already gone. I ran my hands over his eyes closing them permanently.

Finley moved up behind me, jerking me off the ground. "You are making this worse," he said. I tried to get away from him, but he held me tightly. "I love you, Glory, but you have to go now."

"You told him," I grunted.

"I did not," Finley said. "He has taken away all of my privileges and assigned me a wife."

"Oh, that's so horrible," I scoffed.

"She is Summer," Finley said. "She will take over for her mother which means I will have to spend the rest of my life in that blazing hell hole."

Finley hated Summer with a passion. Many a Summer maiden had thrown themselves at him, but he wouldn't touch them. My father knew it, too.

Before we could speak again, the Harpies pulled me from his arms. I looked to my father who kept his eyes on the Great Sword as they dragged me out of the room. Once we reached an earthen hallway with the intertwining roots above, the harpies released me with a shove to the ground.

As I stood up, I realized that my father had joined us.

"What do you want?" I snarled at him.

"You will always be my daughter," he said.

"Go fuck your harem, Father. Maybe you will have another

149

daughter, because as far as I am concerned, you are dead to me," I said.

"I would have lost the kingdom had I stood up for you. *You* put me in this difficult spot," he said.

"Really? So, your daughter isn't as important as your kingdom. Great. I'm ready to leave," I said. My body was already shaking from the anger and anxiety. I needed to cry, but not there.

"Gloriana, I did everything that I could do to save you," he said.

"You are the KING! What good is it being a king if you cannot tell your people what to do?" I bellowed.

"Being a king sometimes means knowing the difference between a lost cause and a losing situation," he explained. "Keeping you here was a lost cause, but while you are exiled, you are at least alive. A losing situation."

"Cut your losses, Daddy," I said. I'd only called him Daddy when I was much younger. The word stung, and I could see it in his eyes.

"THAT PAIN WAS the last I'd seen of my father until he arrived in Shady Grove to bail me out of jail," I said.

"He could have saved you," Levi said.

"I have always thought so, but what would have been the cost. Look at Winter now with his death. It's being ruled by a tyrant and usurper that has threatened to destroy the veil."

"Would you give up your children to win it back?" he asked.

"Absolutely not," I said, immediately.

"That makes you very different from him, and I think he knew that," Levi said.

"Perhaps."

"And Cohen?"

"He was forsaken. I don't even know what they did with his body. I used to visit the forest where he and I met, just to remind myself of how love tore out my heart and ripped me from my family. It was like I could feel him there. After a while, I didn't go back. I wanted to forget it all and I swore I'd never fall again. Then I did. Now Dylan is gone too. But it is different, I don't want to forget him. Either of them," I said.

"You never forgot," Levi said.

"Never."

Levi joined me on the couch, and I curled up in his arms. We fell asleep like that which was what I needed more than anything else.

CHAPTER NINETEEN

LEVI JERKED UP ON THE COUCH, CAUSING ME TO ROLL OFF ONTO THE floor.

"Oh, shit, Grace!" he said, reaching down to me.

"I'm fine. What's wrong?" I asked.

"The ward is breached. Stay here with the kids," he said, then disappeared.

"*What the fuck!*" I said

"*Stay there!*"

I got up and hurried down the hallway to Callum's room. Lightly tapping on the door, I heard him rustling around in the bed, then he opened the door. His blonde hair jutted out wildly.

"Mom, what's wrong?" he asked.

"Levi just left. The ward was breached. I wanted someone else to be awake if we had any problems," I said.

"Sure. I'll start a pot of coffee," he said.

"Thank you, Callum," I said.

"No need to thank me. We are family," he said.

I beamed with pride when he said it. I hustled upstairs to peek in on Aydan, who was sprawled across his bed. He never slept under the covers because he said it was too hot. I suppose he got that from his father.

When I checked on Winnie, Bramble and Briar rushed to the door. I motioned for them to come into the hallway.

"My Queen, you look distressed," Bramble whispered. I wasn't sure how he did it, but his voice was even shrill as a whisper.

"Levi had to go out. Stay with Winnie and protect her. Keep Rufus in there with you," I said. I had noticed the dog sleeping on the end of the bed. He barely lifted his head when I looked in on her.

"We will protect her, My Queen," Briar said.

I knew Brownies had magic, but I didn't know what they could possibly do to an intruder, but if Bramble started talking, it would be like an alarm going off for me.

"Thank you," I said, cracking the door open for them. They flew back inside and settled into the dollhouse they called home.

"*Levi!*"

"*Astor and Tennyson are with me. Someone is definitely here. We are tracking him,*" he said.

"*Please be careful,*" I pleaded.

"*Always.*"

Waiting was agony. I paced the living room floor to the kitchen so many times that I'd almost started a rut in the flooring. Callum fixed me a cup of coffee. I took one sip, then set it down. It was cold now. Levi had checked in a couple of times saying they were on the trail of someone. He insisted that I remain in the house.

"Since when do I let anyone tell me what to do?" I said, grabbing my keys.

"Mom, please stay," Callum said.

"But…" I started to protest, but the look in his eyes begging me to stay broke me. This was what it was like to be a mom. Sometimes I had to stay behind. I hated it, but wouldn't change it. I sat my keys down, then plopped down on the couch with a huff.

Callum refreshed my coffee and handed it to me. I looked down in the cup to see swirling sparkles.

"Where did you learn to do that?" I asked.

"Nestor gave Levi some of the coffee to have here at the house for special occasions," Callum said.

"I don't even know what goes on in my own house," I groaned.

He chuckled at me.

And we waited.

For an hour. Then two.

Finally, I had enough.

"I don't know where you are, but I'm coming to you," I told Levi.

I felt his presence suddenly appear outside. Two sets of footsteps rattled on the wooden front porch. Levi entered with a man I didn't expect to see.

"Seamus?"

"Well, there she is. The most beautiful woman I've ever seen," he said, walking up to me. He took my hand, kissed the top of it, then gave me a slight bow. "It is a pleasure to see you again."

"What are you doing here?" I asked.

"Tennyson had me checking on a few things. He pays well, and I didn't realize that the entire town was surrounded by a ward. It seems I triggered quite the panic," he said.

"You had to know we had protections," I said.

"Well, perhaps, and guess what? They work." He laughed. Levi stood behind him with his arms crossed.

"What's wrong?" I asked.

"You were leaving," he said.

"Levi Rearden, this is my town, my house, and I will do what I want," I said.

He shook his head at me, refusing to argue. Wanker. He had me worried and I wanted him to argue with me.

"I'm sorry to have alarmed you, Grace," Seamus said.

"Would you like some coffee?" Callum asked.

"Seamus, this is Callum, my son," I said. Callum beamed.

"A fine-looking young man. I didn't realize you had two sons," Seamus said.

"I'm adopted," Callum replied handing Seamus a cup of coffee.

"Interesting. I don't believe I've ever met a fairy that adopted so many children. I've heard of fairies providing protection for cities and towns, but never individuals. Unless we are talking about muses," Seamus said, taking a seat in the living room. I sat with him, but Levi remained standing. Good. We needed to have a fight. Sex was always better after a fight.

"I'm different," I said.

"That you are. I am pleased that we met in Las Vegas, and I hope that we can have a profitable relationship," Seamus said, while twirling a ring on his finger. Through my sight, I could see that each of his adornments had magical powers. Not just the rings, but his leather bracelets, earrings, and necklace. One of the bracelets caught my eye.

"That bracelet. The one with the spiral. What does it do?" I asked.

He touched the one I was indicating and smiled. "This one has healing properties. I can get shot or some bloke can shove a sword in me, and I heal up quickly. It was given to me by a druid." His eyes flicked to Levi and back when he mentioned the sword. I supposed there must have been some sort of confrontation.

Dawn had arrived and the room slowly filled with light. Seamus, stood up, dusted off nothing from his double-breasted wool coat, and said, "It's been a pleasure, but I do not have a desire to stay here long. I'm sure I might have a few enemies here. I'm sure Levi and Tennyson will tell you about the information that I procured for them."

"I don't know what it was, but I thank you for your help," I said.

"No need to thank me, Beautiful. I was paid." He grinned as he walked to the front door. Levi opened it for him. He looked back at me, then winked. I was sure the man was part devil. Considering that he was a blood sucker, it wasn't far from the truth.

"I'm going to see him to the border," Levi said.

"Then you will come home and tell me what the fuck is going on," I said.

"Then I will come home," he replied.

"Levi," I said. He froze in place at the door.

"What?"

I walked up and kissed him on the cheek. The tension in his face relaxed and his eyelids lowered. "Be careful," I said, rubbing it in. He was being a twat, and I decided to make him feel bad about it.

"I will."

He left with Seamus through a portal that he made with the sword. I could see Tennyson's house through the glittering circle. It closed as quickly as it had opened right after they passed through it.

When I looked back to Callum, he was asleep in the recliner. I picked up a blanket and covered him with it. He shifted in the seat, but didn't wake up.

I laid down on the couch to get a few moments rest until the house exploded with waking children, brownies, and a dog.

Two seconds. I swear I was laying down for a total of two seconds. Maybe one and a half.

"Momma, can I come downstairs?" Winnie asked.

"Sure. Come on down," I said.

Callum raised up from the recliner. "Oh, crap. I fell asleep."

"It's fine. Go on back to your room and rest," I suggested.

"Okay. Thanks, Mom. Mornin' Winnie," he said as Winnie came down the stairs with Rufus, Bramble, and Briar.

"Hey," she said simply. "Mom, what's for breakfast?"

"Cereal," I replied.

She groaned but made her way to the kitchen. I joined her. We were munching on cinnamon cereal when Levi came back home. He took one look at me, then marched upstairs like we weren't even in the kitchen.

"Uh, oh. He's mad. What did you do?" Winnie asked.

"I don't know, but I'm about to find out," I said, setting my cereal down to follow him.

When I got upstairs his door was open, but he wasn't inside. I looked into my room, and he was standing there with his arms crossed. I stepped inside and prepared myself for whatever he had to say.

CHAPTER TWENTY

INSTEAD OF SPEAKING, I DECIDED TO WAIT HIM OUT. HE HUFFED, then began.

"Tennyson had Seamus checking on a location for your mother and if there are other possible fairies. He didn't find them, but he did find an operation out of Steelshore that alarmed us. Tashi was right. Someone is trafficking fairies in and out of the town," he said.

"Fairy trafficking has been going on for ages," I said.

"In our state!" Levi said. He wasn't mad at me. Thank the stars.

"We are stretched thin preparing for war. What can we do?" I asked.

"We can't. That's the problem," he said.

"We need to make our moves," I said. "Like yesterday."

"Yes. We are ready, Grace. Are you?"

"I think so."

"Then we need to get together with the knights and decide what the plan is going forward," he said, staring up into the gaping hole in the ceiling. "And I'll fix this today."

"I thought you were mad at me," I admitted.

"I'm just mad." Brood.

I walked up to him and wrapped my arms around his waist. He hugged me back tightly.

"Our life is never going to be normal. If it isn't a squirrel plague, it will be witches in red cloaks. We just gotta roll with the punches."

"I'm going to punch something," he huffed. "Grace, if I ask you to stay behind, it's because I know I don't need you there. If it had gotten bad, I would have called for you. I'm here to help you. At the time, staying with the kids was more important. If they are the reason we are doing this, they should be protected."

"I know. It's just that I feel like it's my job to be out there."

"It's *our* job," he replied.

"So, you were mad at me," I teased.

"Maybe a little. You can be rather frustrating," he said.

"Who me?"

He just laughed instead of answering. "I'll go down to the last few houses we put up for Babineau. I think there was some sheetrock left over."

"You don't have to do that now."

"Yes, I do, because you see that bed. You and me are going to be in it! Soon!" he said, pointing at the bed covered in sheetrock and insulation from the attic. "Fucking squirrels."

"One," I said.

"Oh, no you don't! I've got about a hundred of those to catch up with you."

"Just a hundred?"

"Thousands."

NESTOR CALLED SAYING that Tashi and Mike had produced the beer needed to attract the squirrels. To say that I was skeptical about the whole thing would be putting it lightly. We loaded up the kids and headed into town. The snow had mostly thawed leaving only small patches in the shadows.

"Can you make it snow again, Mom?" Winnie asked.

"Why?"

"Because it's fun to play in, but it melted around me so quickly," she said.

"I'm not sure I can produce snow cold enough not to melt around you."

She sighed deeply. The trials of being a phoenix.

"That's okay. At least when I throw a snowball at you, it goes away before it even hits you," Aydan said.

"You better not throw snowballs at me," Winnie warned.

"You just wait. I'll find a way to get you," Aydan teased.

"Put rocks in them," Callum said.

"Callum!" I exclaimed.

"She's tough. She can take it," Callum replied.

"Rocks. Hmmm," Winnie said.

"No, ma'am." Mom voice.

"Ooookay," she huffed. "Callum, bad idea."

"Ooookay," he mocked her.

"So, we get to meet the Yeti?" Aydan asked.

"Yep. He's alright. I guess. I don't know any other of his kind," I said.

"This beer thing is going to work?" Callum asked.

"I hope," I replied.

"It will," Levi said with confidence. At least one of us had it.

Perhaps we had found a solution, but my concern was who actually sent the damn things in the first place. Levi and I had discussed it while he patched up the ceiling in the bedroom. He kept calling it our bedroom. I supposed he was moving in. It was time. We weren't kidding anyone. Everyone in the house knew we were together, just not the way either of us wanted to be.

"Hey Winnie, what do you get when you cross a Yeti with a vampire?" Callum asked.

"I dunno. What?"

"Frostbite."

She giggled, so he continued.

"What do you get when you cross a yeti with a kangaroo?"

"A kangaroo?"

"Fur coat with pockets," he answered.

She laughed more, and we started laughing at her.

"What do you call a yeti with a 6 pack?" Callum asked.

Winnie laughed so hard she couldn't answer him.

"An abdominal snowman," he answered.

"That's funny," Levi said.

It was just corny enough to be funny, and we needed the laughs.

"When did you become the comedian?" I asked.

"Every family needs one," Callum answered.

Aydan tried not to laugh by shaking his head. Callum poked him in the side. "Stop!" Aydan protested.

"Laugh! You know it's funny!" Callum insisted.

Levi's fingers entwined with mine as we listened to the kids in the back of the truck. Callum continued to tell jokes to get Aydan to laugh. Then finally he got him.

"What do you call a yeti dance?"

"What?" Winnie asked.

"A Snow Ball."

"I've been to one of those actually," I said.

Aydan finally cracked up and laughed the rest of the way.

When we got to the bar, Callum walked up close to me. "Hey, Mom?"

"Yeah?"

"What do you call a yeti in a whorehouse?" he asked.

I grinned. This joke was just for me. "I don't know, Callum. Please enlighten me."

"Him-a-layin'."

Groan.

I laughed anyway. "Who knew you were so silly?"

"I did," he said.

"Come on, you can tell them to Tashi," I said.

"I don't know if that is a good idea," he said.

"Some big bad wolf you are," I said. "He knows you guys chased him. He thought it was fun, and I'll bet he will love your jokes."

"We'll see," he said.

~

YOU WOULD HAVE THOUGHT there was a comedy show inside Hot Tin when we arrived. Nestor, Mike, and Tashi were all laughing and slapping their knees. The giggles from my crew continued seeing them laugh.

"See, Callum. You have an audience," I said.

"Audience for what?" Nestor asked.

"It's seems our White Wolf is quite the comedian," I said.

"Mom," Callum groaned.

"I love a good joke," Tashi exclaimed. "Try them out on me, Little Wolf."

"Um," Callum said.

The men at the bar waited with raised eyebrows.

"Go ahead," I said. "By the way, these are my children, Callum, Aydan, and Winnie."

"Hi," Winnie said, raising a quick hand for a wave. The big hairy beast intimidated her. I just hoped she didn't set all that hair on fire.

"They aren't funny," Aydan proclaimed.

"You were laughing in the truck," Levi reminded him.

"Yeah, well, that's because all of you were laughing," Aydan protested.

"Laughter by peer pressure. I'm such a bad mom." I laughed, nudging Callum.

"Well, what do you call it when you mix a yeti and a kangaroo?" Callum muttered.

"Oh! Tell me!" Tashi exclaimed eagerly.

"A fur coat with pockets," Callum said covering his eyes.

Tashi began to laugh. A little at first, then it erupted inside the small bar. Mike chuckled along with Nestor, and I grinned for Callum's bravery. He raised his chin and told the rest of his jokes minus the whorehouse joke. For some reason, that one was reserved for me.

The kids migrated to the pool table to play while we talked. Nestor hung a closed sign on the front door. Our knights joined us so we could discuss our response to the squirrels, but also, my desire to push our attack on Winter. The two seemed like completely different issues, but in the grand scheme, the plague of bushy-tailed rodents had the town's focus when it needed to be on the fight. It worried me that Brockton was about to make a move on us again, even though all of Tennyson's intelligence pointed to no movement on the Winter front.

"The squirrels are from summer," I said out loud.

Levi looked up from his conversation with Troy who had arrived with Mark. Instead of running off to play with Winnie, Mark stayed close to his father. Winnie didn't seem to notice since Luther brought Soraya with him, and the two girls were busy lining the pool balls for the boys to knock them around the table.

"Why do you think that?" Levi asked.

"If Brock hasn't moved, then it has to be Rhiannon," I said.

"That makes sense," Tashi said. "Squirrels move about in the winter, especially in the southern areas of this land, but they are summer creatures."

"Why would she make a move on us?" Troy asked.

"Stephanie. Mostly the helm," I said. "Perhaps she's trying to protect the veil, but I am willing to bet that she wants to be the one to control it."

"We've got to get that damn thing off her head," Levi said.

"I haven't found anything that says we can take it off," Tennyson offered. "I've searched all my sources and contacts. No one seems to know."

"I bet there are books in the library at home," Finley said.

"No! You are not going there," I said, knowing what he was implying.

"I can get in and out," Finley insisted.

"No," I repeated.

"She's right. We need you here," Tennyson offered. "We will find another way."

"If they are Summer, I can control them," Astor offered.

"Can you? I thought you didn't do magic?" I said, twiddling my fingers at him.

He grinned. "I refrain, but I have been taught some things," he admitted.

"If they are Summer, then your mother is controlling them. Can you overpower that?" I asked.

"I might not be able to, but if we dose them with the brew, then lead them out of town, it just might work. I think if we get them beyond the ward, we will be safe from the buggers," Astor said.

"We need to squash this. I'm tired of waiting. It's time to move," I huffed. I stood from my chair and paced the room. No one spoke as the temperature dropped in the bar. The children stopped their games as Levi watched me intently. "This has gone on long enough. This world has more problems than just my wayward uncle in Winter. We cannot address those problems until he is overthrown. I know it isn't going to happen tonight, but I'm telling all of you right now. It happens. And it better happen soon."

Tennyson was the brave soul to speak. "Grace, we are making plans, but taking Winter isn't going to be simple now that he's had time to set up roots there. I understand that we couldn't have moved any sooner, and that your father got caught off guard with all of this, but we can't go in there without a plan."

"How long? What more do you have to do?" I asked.

"A couple of months. The fighters need more training. We have to finish the weapons," he explained.

I walked over to his table and leaned over it. "I want it done yesterday."

Tennyson Schuyler wasn't used to anyone telling him what to do. Not since he was a knight in my father's court. I respected his abilities and connections, but he needed to know my intensity. Perhaps I just needed to get laid. My eyes flicked to Levi who fought a grin. Fucking bard.

"I understand. Give me two weeks," Tennyson said. He didn't push back at all. Maybe I finally had the hang of this ruling thing. When I looked in his eyes, I saw it. He was proud of me like my father should have been. Maybe he would have been.

After telling Levi about my story with Cohen, I realized that Tennyson had been leading the same life Cohen had chosen. A life away from the Otherworld. Separated from the assurance of eternal life. Mingling with humans. Tennyson had succeeded, and I had derailed Cohen. And perhaps Jeremiah, too.

"Where is Caiaphus?" I asked.

"I haven't seen him lately, but he keeps to himself," Astor said. "I check on him every once in a while."

"Why?" Tennyson asked.

"I need to know if he knew someone," I said. "It's unrelated to the squirrels and the war."

"Who?" Tennyson persisted. My eyes darted to Levi who nodded.

"Cohen," I said.

"Who is Cohen?" Troy asked.

"A good man," Tennyson said. "Why would you ask Caiaphus about him?"

"Because I think that maybe Jeremiah was his friend and maybe Cohen was Sanhedrin," I said. "He had a robe. A cleric's robe."

"I'm glad that you are finally talking about him. He was a good man and should not be forgotten," Tennyson said. "But I can answer your questions."

"I'll never forget him," I said.

Astor clearly knew who I was talking about, but Troy was still confused. Luther listened in with no expression on his face.

"Jeremiah and Cohen were friends. The Sanhedrin are summer fairies. In the early days, they were guided by Summer. By Rhiannon. In later days, the factions split, even before this recent split. But when Cohen was alive, there was a movement to include some exiled Winter fairies in their order. Jeremiah was recruiting Cohen. However, his relationship with you made that impossible. Once Jeremiah realized that Cohen wouldn't give you up, he moved on, but not before you healed him which set into motion something that has played out over hundreds of years. That kindness has brought you to this place, because Jeremiah brought you to this place. So, no, Cohen was not Sanhedrin," Tennyson said.

"How do you know this?" I asked.

"Because they tried to recruit me as well. Cohen and I disagreed on the matter. However, the last letter I received from him talked about meeting a fairy woman and that his opinion of Winter exiles had changed. Your father wasn't mad at Cohen because he had Excalibur, but that he might use it against Winter fairies. Even exiled ones. You changed his mind on that, but your father's wrath did not change," Tennyson said.

"And my love for him cost him his life," I said quietly. Troy questioned me without saying a word. "I was banished from the Otherworld, not for loving many men. I loved one man. An exile that my father hated."

"His name was Cohen?" Troy asked.

"No, but it is what he wanted me to call him. His name is forbidden from every fairy tongue. No one here can say it. Something that I will change when we take back Winter." This too caused Tennyson to smile. Again, he approved, and although his approval wasn't something I sought out, I was very grateful to have it.

"I believe I could say the name," Luther said.

"Probably," I replied.

"If we fail, I promise to speak it for you," Luther added.

"Damn you, Demon. Don't make me cry," I said.

"Well, I say we rid this town of some varmints and take back the Otherworld," Levi said with a smile which lightened the mood.

"I'm all for that. The bastards ate through my back porch," Astor said.

"What do you need to do to get them here?" I asked Astor.

"I'm not completely sure. I might have to get some advice on that one," he said. "Magic isn't my thing."

"Riley would know," Finley, who had kept quiet during the Cohen discussion, offered.

"I actually think that is a good idea. With her connection to Summer and the witches, she is the one who could help you," I said.

Finley picked up his cell phone to make the call.

Tashi and Nestor spoke quietly about microbrewing beer, and if Tashi decided to stay, Nestor promised to serve his brew at Hot Tin. When I sat down at the bar, Nestor automatically served me a cup of coffee which I sipped slowly. Levi moved up next to me, shielding me from the rest of the conversation.

"Are you okay?" he asked.

"Yeah, why?"

"A lot just happened right there and you aren't blocking me, but you feel a little distant," he said.

"I'm not blocking you. I'm blocking everything. I don't have time to mull over the past," I said.

"One day we will. I'll write it all down. His story will be told," Levi said.

"My father knew you would be right for me. He gave you the bard gifts, but I have to think that you deserved them. That you were perfect to receive them," I mused.

"Are you saying I'm perfect for you, Grace?" he asked.

"I'm just saying you are perfect," I replied.

"I think that's the most wonderful thing you've ever said to me."

"Don't get used to it."

He hugged me tightly and kissed my cheek. "I wouldn't dare."

AS WE RODE HOME, Levi wanted to know about Finley and what Father did to him after he found out about Cohen.

"I assume your father knew that Finley knew about Cohen?"

"He did. Finley was stripped of his title as King's son or King. His lands were given to our other brothers, and Father made him the leader of his guard. So, in the past when I've called Finley 'Prince' it has been a dig at him. Brothers and sisters do those things. He started the whole Glory business. Outside of him, Cohen, you, and Dylan, no one else has called me that. I don't mind it. But it brings back memories."

"Focus on the good ones."

"The bad ones overshadow it. I know I'll never be able to make it up to him."

"That's not true. I think being Queen of the Exiles would have pleased him. He was dedicated to that principle. I know that Tennyson admires you for it."

"He would have liked it, mainly because if it had come up back then, I would have cursed him."

"Always the foul mouth."

"Always."

The lights on the dashboard illuminated his face as he drove us home. A smile stayed fixed upon it.

"We have a date in the morning," he said.

"No, we have to wrangle squirrels in the morning," I replied.

"That's later on. I'm taking you to breakfast. Callum has agreed to be on cereal duty in the morning," Levi said.

"Yep," Callum confirmed.

Looking over my shoulder, I saw Winnie leaned over asleep next to him. Aydan stared out into the night, but he seemed to be content.

"Thank you, Callum."

CHAPTER TWENTY-ONE

When we arrived home, the power was out again. Troy called to tell us that they were working on getting it restored. Levi started a fire in the fireplace while Aydan and Callum got blankets for all of us to sleep downstairs. I kissed all of them goodnight, then curled up with Levi on the couch.

The next morning the lights had returned. Levi and I took separate showers before we headed out for our breakfast date. Callum already had bowls of cereal made up for everyone as they started to stir.

"Stay here. After breakfast we will be summoning the squirrels. The centaurs will be outside and Nestor will be here soon. Cool?" Levi asked.

"We've got it," Aydan replied.

I'd chosen jeans and a black sweater with a slouchy shoulder. It showed off the strap of my lacy black bra underneath. If we were going on a date, I had to tempt him somehow.

"Ready?" Levi asked.

"This outfit okay?" I asked back.

"It's perfect," he replied as he leaned down to kiss the bare part of my shoulder. I was pretty sure that he was tempting me more than I was him. He took my hand, and instead of driving, as soon as we hit the front porch, he skipped us to the front door of the diner.

When we stepped inside, the normally bustling cafe was silent. Betty stood behind the counter with her back to us. She turned around to greet us with a bright smile.

"Well, there you are. I was beginning to think you weren't coming," she said.

"Kinda slow today?" I asked.

"No, the mayor declared that the businesses in town should be closed today for the extermination of our furry visitors. However, he asked for a private breakfast, and heavens knows I can't tell that handsome face no," she replied.

"Private breakfast?" I asked, looking at him.

"Yep," he replied, leading me to a stool at the center of the counter.

"What will it be?" Betty asked, taking the pen from behind her ear to tap it on her order pad.

"I want my usual with coffee," Levi said. "What about you, Grace?"

"I'll have eggs, bacon, and coffee," I said.

"We are fresh out of eggs," she said with a tsk. "This winter weather has been rough on our inventory."

"Okay, well, what about pancakes?" I asked.

"Nope. Sorry. No pancakes."

I saw were this was going, and I had no choice but to succumb to the will of Levi Readen. "I'll have what he's having," I grunted.

"Great choice!" Betty exclaimed.

I shook my head at the non-sense. Luther grinned at me through the service window. He lifted his hand to reveal an egg. I smirked at him, then turned my smirk to Levi.

"What?" He laughed.

"You think you are cute."

"Oh, honey. I'm not cute. I'm fucking handsome."

I died laughing at him. Betty giggled as she served us coffee. "Your order will be right up. I'm gonna leave the pot here. You kids have fun."

"Huh?"

"After Luther cooks our breakfast, they are going to head over to Hot Tin for a bit giving us a little time to eat in private," Levi explained.

"Oh," I replied. Surely, he didn't expect us to have sex in the diner. It wasn't how I imagined our first time, but who knew what he had in his imagination. Either way, I knew I'd love it.

Betty approached us with one covered plate. "Sorry, Grace. We only had enough for one plate. Guess you will have to share." She grinned as she sat the plate in front of us. Luther appeared from the kitchen sans apron.

"Hope y'all enjoy it," he said with a warm smile.

As they walked out the door, he patted her on the ass.

"Luther Harris! My stars! We are in public. Behave yourself!"

His deep chuckle faded as the door closed behind them leaving Levi and I alone.

"You do the honors," he said.

"Whatever," I said, as I grabbed the handle on the cover.

"No! Not whatever. Be nice, Grace," he said, slipping his hand over mine to prevent me from looking under it.

"This is me being nice."

"You can do better."

I grunted, then tugged at the lid. He released my hand, and I lifted the lid. Steam poured out from under it revealing a large plate of biscuits and gravy.

It had to be gravy.

"Levi."

"Grace, will you share your gravy with me?"

How utterly corny. Adorable. Endearing. Damn. I really did love him.

~

"HOLD ON, ONE FUCKING MINUTE," I said. "Like it just hit you then?"

"Yeah," she shrugged. "I mean. I said I love you, but I felt the full impact of it staring at a plate of steaming gravy biscuits."

"Really?"

"I loved you, Levi. Before then, but something about that moment stuck with me. It wasn't because Dylan dreamed it or because of some cosmic fate. Hell, it had nothing to do with my father and his schemes. It had everything to do with what a sincere and loving man you were. Are."

I got up from the table where I had been typing and crossed the room to her. She tried to run from me when I got close, but I pulled her back to me.

"Damn. I need gravy now after that speech," I said. She shivered at my touch and the tone of my voice.

"Levi Rearden, git your ass back over to the chair and finish this part of the story!" she demanded. I tried to kiss her, but she moved her face. My lips planted on her cheek, so I turned up the tingle sending the waves of our attraction through her body. "My stars, Levi. Stop."

I relented and released her from my hold. "You better hurry up! Get to the end of this."

She pointed at the laptop sitting on the dining room table. I shuffled back over, then sat down in my chair. I had to adjust my jeans a couple of times to get comfortable. She watched me with a knowing grin that I wanted to smack off of her face.

Aggravating.

Infuriating.

Completely fuckable woman.

Tonight, there would be guitar.

～

"I'M AWFULLY HUNGRY," he said. "But I think this time, I'll share."

He had no bedroom ideas. I felt that from him. Bless his little heart, he just wanted to have a date. I recalled the Valentine's date with Riley, and how in the end they both got what they wanted. I was damn glad I'd be getting what I wanted from him.

"You better share." I cut off a piece of biscuit, twirling it in the gravy. Ignoring the connotation, the plate of biscuits looked fantastic. They tasted even better.

"Good?"

"So good. Thank you, Levi."

"I wanted you to know that even though I'm completely frustrated that just being with you is enough for me."

"You are too human sometimes."

"That sounded like an insult."

"Insult. Compliment. Kinda in the middle."

"I'll take it."

"Levi?"

"Huh?" He lifted a fork full of biscuit, loading it into his mouth.

"What's your middle name?"

The human left his eyes and was replaced with an evil demon. He chewed on his biscuit, taking his time, then said, "I'm not going to tell you."

I slapped his shoulder. "Pain in the ass!"

"Fine. I'll take back my gravy!" He slid the plate out of my reach.

"You better give me that gravy!" I shouted.

"Oh, you want to do it here? I hadn't thought of that, but I suppose we could." He grinned like a possum sitting in a trash can full of leftovers. He wrapped his arm around me, pulling me to him.

"No! Not here!" I exclaimed.

"If I didn't know better, Grace Ann, I'd think you were scared of swappin' gravy with me," he said.

"I am not!"

He stopped playing with me. "Wait. Are you?"

"No."

"Nervous?"

"No."

"Liar! What the hell? Why are you scared?"

"It's not fear! Its..."

"It's what?"

What was it? There was something there. The fairy inside me told me to shut my mouth and fuck him right here. I told her to shut-up, so I could think. I closed my eyes. Levi's hand found my neck and his thumb stroked my lower cheek. There was a timidity with Levi that I hadn't experienced before with any other conquest. Perhaps it was because Levi wasn't a conquest. His heart was already mine. He had just been waiting on me. I had pursued every man, including Dylan. Levi had been silently, persistently courting me. A position that I had never been in, and I'd been in a lot of positions.

"You are different than all the others."

"Well, damn. I'd hope so," he said, not understanding.

"No. It's hard to explain, but I didn't have to seduce you. You've been here waiting on me. It's usually the other way around for me."

His forehead wrinkled as he took in my words. "There were others. Kady. Riley."

"Dylan."

"Not the same."

"Why?"

"Because you loved Dylan and he loved you."

"You loved them, right?"

"Not like I loved you. Kady was right all along. I refused to admit it. I'd never be complete until I had you."

"Well, fuck," I whispered.

"That's the idea." He grinned. "What is that? Six? Seven?"

I pinched him in the side, and he howled like a baby. "That fucking hurt!"

"Two!" I yelled at him as I jumped up off my seat.

He tried to grab me, but I slipped out of his grasp. He fell to the floor with a thud.

"Damn!"

"Oh! Are you okay?"

He stopped his pretending to try and grab me. I dodged him and ran out of the diner. He was hot on my heels as I ran for the Hot Tin. I made it to the door just as he caught me. I spun around to face him with his arms encasing me. I finally felt like I was exactly where I belonged. We were both breathing hard, but he took my breath away with a long, soft kiss.

"Gotcha," he whispered.

"I'm yours," I replied.

Someone opened the door behind me, and we tumbled into the bar. I looked up into the eyes of our very own Alpha werewolf.

"What are y'all doing?" Troy asked, looking down at us.

"Swappin' gravy," I replied.

Levi rolled over on the floor, laughing and holding his side.

"I'm sorry I asked," Troy said, offering to help me up. Levi jumped up, nudging Troy out of the way. He helped me stand, and we looked into the room of our friends. The light of laughter and happiness filled their eyes and faces.

"Some of us are trying to save this city from a plague of rodents!" Jenny teased.

"And some of us are here to help. Not Levi. I meant me," I replied as Levi stepped behind me.

Chuckles filled the room. Just before everyone returned to their preparations, Levi leaned in and kissed *that* spot on my neck. The same spot he always touched. Maybe it was a love-talker thing, but it was the same spot that Cohen used to own me too. Desire and memory of desire mingled, and I suddenly wanted to just exterminate the squirrels. It would be quicker.

CHAPTER TWENTY-TWO

RILEY, WENDY, AND KADY PREPARED A LARGE CHALK CIRCLE IN THE
Food Mart parking lot. A summoning circle. The demons were
bright-eyed and bushy-tailed menaces. A large circle framed a
slightly smaller circle. On the inside of the circle, a sun with eight
rays. Four pointed to the points on a compass. The other four filled
the gaps. Kady sat on the asphalt finishing up the sun with a box of
kid's sidewalk chalk.

"I guess the materials used to make the circle don't matter?" I
asked.

She looked up to me with a smile. "No. The magic is what
matters. The circle operates only when imbued with power."

"Maybe we should have Winnie power it," I suggested.

She laughed. "If she had been trained, I'm sure it would work
for her."

"Are you finished?" I asked.

"Yep. Wendy and Riley are gathering a few things to put inside
the circle," she replied.

"Like?"

"Things to entice the demons. Sorry, I know they are squirrels,
but they ate holes in my favorite sweater that my dad gave me."

"How is your dad?" I asked. It had been a while since I had seen Matthew Rayburn. Sometimes I forgot that Cletus and Tater weren't the only humans still left in Shady Grove.

"He's better. Getting used to moving around the house. I think he misses doing Sunday services at the church," she said.

"We should keep having them. I know we have all been busy with the happenings of late and it's not going to get any better, but coming together as a community is important," I replied.

"He will be excited to hear that, Grace. You should visit him. He asks about you all the time. He worried that Dylan's death would be a blow to you, but I told him that you have continued on with your children."

"For my children."

"And Levi?"

"Levi is a bonus."

She smiled. "At one time, I might have agreed with you."

"I'm glad you don't now."

"No, Caleb is fantastic. We are getting married."

"Congratulations! That's wonderful."

"Thank you. I better get this finished," she said.

I moved away as she made the final touches on her artwork. Riley and Wendy were organizing items on the tailgate of Riley's truck. Finley leaned next to it in a pair of jeans and a t-shirt. All he needed was a cowboy hat, and he might just fit in with his platinum locks.

Riley filled four bowls with items. One was filled with several cans of mixed nuts that Levi had swiped from Nestor's bar stash. Another bowl was filled with greens like kale and lettuce. The third bowl was filled with fresh fruits like blackberries, strawberries, and grapes. In the final container, a mix of mushrooms piled up to the top edge.

"Want to give me a hand, Grace?" she asked.

"I'll get it," Finley piped up taking two of the bowls.

"Thanks, Finley," she said, beaming at him. Perhaps she did love him. It wasn't my place to question it. If she hurt him, then I could rip her throat out. "Thanks, anyway, Grace."

"Oh, huh? Oh, no problem," I said, as her voice jarred me out of my momentary darkness.

I watched them place the bowls in the voids inside the circle. Then Tashi came up to each bowl with his metal backpack. Taking a spout that connected to the side, he poured amber liquid over each bowl of food, ruining perfectly good snacks.

"I like beer and peanuts," Levi said, sneaking up behind me.

"You would. That's nasty," I said. "Piss water and nuts."

"Yep, you can get one of those plastic packs of nuts at the store, and just pour them suckers right down into the beer. You gotta let them sit a minute, then it's *so* good," he kept on talking. "You should try it sometime. It might change your opinion of beer."

"I doubt there is anything in this world or below it that could change my opinion of beer," I replied.

"Oh, I bet it would be good with nuts in your whiskey," he teased, carrying it too far.

"You keep your nuts out of my whiskey."

"Can I put them somewhere else?"

I turned around as I slapped his shoulder. "And I'm the vulgar one? Really?"

"I'm not vulgar. I'm just horny," he admitted, wrapping his leg around mine. Humping me like a dog would be a deal breaker.

"Git away from me," I said, shoving him away. He laughed, but didn't try it again.

I caught Jenny watching us. "I'm going to go talk to Jenny. You help them finish this," I said, waving my hand at the circle preparation.

"Yes, ma'am, my Queen," he replied.

When I got over to Jenny, she locked her arm through mine like we were schoolmates. "What are you doing?"

"We need to talk. When this is over, meet me in the salon," she said.

"About what?" I asked.

"I wouldn't ask if it wasn't important," she insisted.

"Alright," I huffed. All I wanted to do was to go home and fuck the king, but it seemed like once again someone else had something planned for my evening.

"We are ready," Riley announced.

All of my knights were there along with the white witches. Tashi, Mike, and Deacon Giles. If Deacon was here, then I was sure that the Yule Lads were probably nearby.

Astor walked up to me. "Mind if I take this one?" he said.

"Not at all," I replied

He stepped into the middle of the gathering, but did not disturb the circle. "What we have built is a simple summoning circle to call to us the Summer creatures. We've offered them snacks. It's our opinion that this is an attack from Summer. However, I believe that I have the power within me to override it. I ask that you stay away from the circle. Do not disturb the creatures as they arrive. The Lads are handing out brooms. Use these to sweep any that stray into the circle before I can activate the trap. Please do not break the circle lines with the brooms, which I'm sure you already know, but just in case. I will read from a text given to me by Riley to summon the creatures to us."

Riley handed him an old book which was opened to the passage. Lamar walked by and offered me a broom, but I shook my head. I wanted to keep my hands free. Who knows who started all of this. Besides, I might need my hands. I felt the hilts of my daggers poking inside my bra. Almost as if they were itching to get out and be used. As Lamar walked away, I saw that his peg leg had been replaced with a broom end. He had an interesting collection of prosthetics, but I dared not ask him about it. The Yule Lads were fairy like the rest of us. Who knew what kinds of interesting toys Lamar had. I didn't need to know that kink.

Levi stepped up beside me. He held Excalibur down in a non-threatening position. Astor looked over to me one last time.

"You got this," I encouraged. He nodded back, then began the summoning.

"By the power of the four directions and four elements, I, Astor Knight, call forth the Summer creatures that have invaded this land. By right, as the son of Rhiannon, I call you to come forth to this place. These offerings I bring: fruit, nuts, greens, and mushrooms. They are here for your delight." Astor's voice boomed in the parking lot and echoed off the trees across the street. We waited, but nothing happened.

"I command thee, servants of Summer. Come forth to this place and present yourselves."

Silence. Astor made the third call.

"I, Astor Knight, demand that the enthralled beings of Summer come here now!"

It sounded like a perfectly good dad voice. He would need that later once his twins were born. Ella stood to the side with her friend Crystal. Ella had bloomed out beautifully. It wouldn't be long before we had another birth. Watching her watching him with pride, I knew that my concerns about Astor fitting in here were unfounded. Shady Grove was where he belonged.

A slight rumble echoed around us, then crescendoed as the parking lot began to fill with hopping and skittering squirrels. Most were bigger than your average varmint. The circle was about twenty feet across, and I hoped it was big enough. The ravagers hit the offerings scarfing them down. When it seemed that all of them had arrived, I would have estimated the count to be close to a thousand. They jumped over each other and crawled around the circle. A few tried to stray, but were quickly swept back to the circle. The last one received the boot of Lamar. Or I should say, the peg broom.

Astor cut his finger with a small dagger that he drew from his hip, then placed it on the circle. It ignited in a bright golden glow. The critters began to swagger as Tashi's brew began to take effect.

"I believe it is your show now, Sir Abominable," Astor said.

Tashi nodded, then reached around for the spout to his backpack. He flipped a switch on the side of the metal contraption, and brought the spout to his lips. With a smile and a wink, he blew into the spout and the backpack erupted into a sound that was a mix of pipe organ and bagpipe. As he played the happy tune, the squirrels turned their attention to him. He circled their entrapment playing his song. They turned with him, completely enthralled by the music. When he passed Astor, he nodded, then the knight swept along the edge of the circle with his foot, breaking the spell. The squirrels spilled out rapidly, congregating around Tashi's feet.

"Well, I'll be damned," I said, staring at the spectacle.

Tashi marched out of the parking lot toward trailer lake and the town's welcome sign. As he passed, the waters stirred with the guardian there. Levi and I moved toward the parade to make sure that the Yeti's efforts weren't disturbed, but the waters calmed as we approached.

"That damn swamp still makes me nervous," I said.

"Me too," Levi replied.

I hadn't realized that Lamar and some of the others had followed us as we moved toward the lake.

"I've got a harpoon peg, Queen Grace. If ya let me, I'll hop in a boat and spear that creature," Lamar said.

"Oh, please, don't do that, Lamar. I don't think she means any harm. We should steer clear of her though," I said.

"Well, if ya change ya mind, let me know," he huffed.

"I will. Thank you, Lamar," I said.

"Harpoon peg," Levi said with a raised eyebrow. "I wonder what other kinds of pegs he has."

"Levi," I hissed.

"What? Like I saw the club one, and he has a harpoon and a broom. Maybe he has a rifle. That would be cool."

"And impractical," I said.

"But cool," Levi persisted. "You thought I was going to say some kinky shit."

"Yes," I replied.

"I was, but I heard your tone." He laughed.

Tashi rounded the corner up ahead of us with his servants in tow. He had explained that he didn't want any of us to follow him so the squirrels wouldn't get distracted if the brew started to wear off. So, we let him go, but I figured we would see him again very soon.

"That seemed too easy," I said as we turned back toward the Food Mart parking lot.

"Maybe sometimes we just win," Levi said.

"Maybe, but we still don't know who did this," I said. About that time, Remy and Tabitha pulled up in his fancy Mercedes. I hadn't seen her in a while, and I wondered if she had been out to visit Amanda and the babies.

She smiled brightly as Levi and I approached. "You do make a lovely couple," she said.

"Why thank you, Tab," Levi replied.

"Where have you been?" I asked.

"Remy and I took a short vacation down to New Orleans," she said.

"I had a few business items to take care of, and I thought I'd take my lovely girlfriend with me. Sorry we didn't check in. I let Tennyson know we were leaving," Remy said. "What's with the circle?"

"Squirrel invasion," I said.

"Yeti brewmaster," Levi added.

"Sounds like fun," Remy said.

"Tons," I replied.

"Did it snow here?" Tabitha asked. "Smells like snow." She wrinkled her nose sniffing the air.

"I made it snow thinking it might deter the squirrel activities, but it didn't work," I said.

"Well, I think it's going to snow again," she said.

I reached out with my senses, and felt a cold front pushing down from the north. She was right. It was going to snow, and I wasn't going to be held responsible this time.

"I think you are right," I smiled. "Look. While you were gone, Amanda had her litter."

"Oh, shit. Are they okay?"

"Yeah, their doc, Wendy, and I delivered them. The first one was breech, but they arrived safely. Three girls," I said.

"Remy, come on. I need to go check on her. When I get done, I'll give you a call, and we can catch up," Tabitha said.

"Sure," I replied.

"Tomorrow," Levi said.

"Huh?"

"We have plans tonight," he added.

"Oh! Sounds like good plans to me," Tabitha said, then climbed back in the car with Remy.

"What plans?" I asked.

"We have to finish our date," he said.

"Jenny wanted to talk to me at the Salon when this was over," I said apologetically.

"It's always something," he huffed.

"It probably won't take long, then I will meet you at home," I said.

"Alright." He kissed me on the cheek before migrating to Tennyson and Astor who were still standing in the parking lot discussing the ritual. I passed them and headed to the small salon in the strip mall that was owned by Chaz Leopold.

When I stepped inside, I found that Chaz along with Jenny, Kady, Wendy, Riley, Betty, and Ella were waiting on me.

"What's going on?" I asked.

"Sit down," Jenny ordered, pointing to the salon chair that Chaz spun around.

"Your throne, my Queen," he said.

"No, seriously. I've got some things to do, and I need to know what you want," I demanded.

Jenny walked over to me and put her arm through mine like before. "Come have a seat. We need to talk to you about something very important."

I sighed deeply, but moved my feet as she dragged me to the chair. As I sat down in it, they gathered around me. I sat silently waiting.

"This is an intervention," Jenny said.

I rolled my eyes and laughed. "What sort of intervention?"

"We are here on behalf of your inner fairy," she continued.

I groaned as Chaz handed me a glass of brown liquid. Lifting it to my nose, I took a deep whiff. Whiskey. At least there was one good thing about this meeting.

CHAPTER TWENTY-THREE

Once the girls had their say, I stepped out of the salon in the early evening. A chill had settled in prior to the approaching cold front. The parking lot was dark, except for a couple of the girls who were getting in their vehicles to go home. The whole point of the meeting had been to delay me.

Sitting in the lot was my truck which I had not driven for the summoning.

"*Truck?*" I asked, reaching out to Levi. I could have just skipped home.

"*Yeah, I thought you might like to drive home,*" he said.

"*Okay,*" I replied.

I climbed into the truck as Troy's cruiser flew into the parking lot. He pulled over next to me, then rolled down his window. I let mine down, too.

"What's wrong?" I asked.

"Come to the jail. Stephanie is threatening to take off the helm if you don't come," he huffed.

"Lead the way," I said. "*Detour.*"

"*What?*"

"*Stephanie is being a twat,*" I said.

187

"*I'll meet you there,*" he said.

It only took a couple of minutes for us to arrive at the jail. Levi waited for us on the front steps. I ran up to him.

"Did you go in?" I asked.

"No, there is a ward. Do you see it?" he asked.

Looking through my sight, I saw the bright green hue surrounding the building. "Can I go through?" I asked.

"If you can't, it will zap you. Hurts like the dickens," he said.

Troy walked straight through it with no problem.

"I'm not walking through it. It's coming down," I said gritting my teeth.

I reached out to the incoming cold front, pulling its dark freeze to me. It swirled above my head in a small vortex of blue lightning and dark clouds. I reached up toward the funnel as its power descended down around me. It sank into my skin fueling my natural Winter magic. I placed my hand on the ward, and it vibrated so hard that it became visible to the human eye. I pressed hard against the barrier. Ice crystals stretched out from my hand, covering the ward. I jerked my hand away breaking the ice. The ward had stuck to the ice and shattered along with it.

"You are scary powerful sometimes," Levi said as we climbed the steps.

"She didn't put up that ward," I said.

"No, probably not. She's lured us out here. Stay alert," I replied.

"Yep," Levi said, drawing Excalibur from its sheath.

When we entered the holding cell room, Stephanie was singing.

"Jack and Jill went up the hill to fetch a pail of water. Jack fell down and broke his crown, and Jill came tumbling after," she sang.

"Stephanie, what is your deal?" I asked.

"Oh, look. It's the Winter Queen who said she wouldn't return to this place except to kill me," she said. "Guess I die today."

She had no idea how much I wish that were true.

"You are marked for death, but the helm stands in the way of that," I said. "But, I'm pretty sure you knew that. Who erected the ward outside? Do you know anything about the squirrels?"

She giggled, then said, "Little Robin Redbreast said, 'Catch me if you can'."

"What the fuck is wrong with her?" I asked.

"Six," Levi muttered. I shook my head. "She's clearly lost her mind."

Stephanie began to skip around in a circle. "Ring-a-round the rosies, pocket full of posies. Ashes! Ashes! We all fall down!" She tumbled to the floor and her head hit last with a thud.

"Open the door," I demanded. Troy quickly produced the key.

Levi wanted to stop me, but he held back. When the iron door slid open, I marched in causing her to scoot back to the wall to avoid me.

"Wait! Wait! Wait!" she screamed.

"Get up!" I yelled, grabbing her by the shirt and yanking her to her feet.

"Please, Grace. Don't kill me. Please, please," she begged.

"You are marked for death. I have no choice but to kill you," I said.

"That is an excuse! Your father could have saved you! Don't be like him!"

"You are not my daughter!" I screamed at the frantic woman. She was a mere shadow of the powerful fairy queen that once kept Dylan's attentions.

"My son. Think of my son," she said.

"You don't give a damn about Devin," I countered.

"I'm a mother. Surely, you understand that!"

"I do understand it, but I don't know how any mother could abandon their child!"

"My mother did. Your father did. Now you are going to make me do it, too!"

"That's hogwash, and you know it," I said, releasing her shirt.

Her body remained plastered to the concrete wall. Her bright eyes looked at me through the slits in the helm. In them I saw the hint of tears. She was genuinely afraid. Slowly, she knelt down before me. She reached up to remove the helmet.

"No!" Levi yelled, rushing to her. His hands pressed down over hers to keep her from taking it off.

"Let me die, Grace. Give me this one mercy."

"Why do you want to die?" I asked. "You just asked me to let you live."

"I need protection. I see now that death is my only option," she said.

"Protection? From Brock?" I asked.

"No, from *her*."

"Rhiannon."

"Yes," she hissed. "She's coming for the helm. Take it from me, Grace. It belongs to you."

"If you take it off of your head, the veil falls between the realms. I cannot let that happen," I said.

She started laughing. "I'm cursed to wear it forever?"

"I don't know. We have been looking for a way," I said.

"The Monarch of a realm can remove it," she said. "So, my mother can take it from me. Brockton couldn't. He's not the King of Winter."

"Grace, you can take it," Levi said. "If she is telling the truth, and I think she is, you can take it. However, it will kill her."

He knew I had to kill her. Part of me wanted to kill her, but the other part heard the plea of a mother who had some connection to her child. There was no way for me to know if she was sincere.

"Yes, Grace, take it from me. It's so heavy," she cried.

"I think he's right, Grace. Take it," Troy urged.

"The risk!" I countered. "If the veil falls!"

"Then it falls, and we deal," Levi said. "But it's not going to fall. That helmet belongs to you! She's a thief, a liar, and a very bad mother."

"Take it from me before she comes. Please. Please." she begged.

She seemed to think Rhiannon would come here for the helm. I grabbed her by the shirt again and asked, "Who put up the ward?"

"I don't know, but you should be afraid. You aren't the only powerful thing in this world or below it, Gloriana. They are coming for you. All of them. They will kill you," she laughed.

"You first," I said, jerking the helm from her head.

Her black hair spilled out of the helmet in maddening tangles. Her breaths labored. Then I heard the snap of fingers behind me. She dissipated into a cloud of icy dust. I stood there, breathing hard and staring at the final remnants of the woman who caused us so much pain.

Levi pulled me backwards away from the place where she died, wrapping me up with his arms from behind. I held my father's helmet in my hands. The power inside of it vibrated. The veil was still intact. I knew, because for the first time in my entire life, I could feel it without touching a tree. It was like a living entity, calling my name. I felt contentment as if it had weathered a great storm, but now it was calm.

"Call Tennyson. Tell him we've got it." I told Levi, who didn't let go of me. He knew how much I loathed executions. He'd done it for me.

"Good riddance," Troy said. "Now I can put my guys on other things."

"Thank you for all you do, Troy. Go home to your kids," I said.

"Goodnight, Grace," he said.

"Vault," Levi said, transporting us to the basement below Mike's vape shop.

We walked inside, and I placed the helmet on a lighted shelf. I stared at the artifact from my father's reign on earth. I had no idea how significant it was. Growing up, I thought my father's responsibilities included throwing parties, having orgies, and producing children. Being a King was so much more.

I had zoned out and didn't realize that Tennyson had arrived.

"She is dead?" he asked.

"Yes," Levi replied.

"Rhiannon won't be happy."

"She didn't care about Stephanie," I said.

"No, she won't be happy that you have the helm. That you control the veil," he said.

"It seems to me, that she of all fairies would want to keep the veil up," I said.

"I'm sure she does, but she wants to control it," Tennyson said. "Good job, Grace. It was a bold move. Exactly what I expect of you."

"You looked at me differently when I talked about making our move," I said.

"Without being condescending, I want you to know that I am proud of you. I know, without a doubt, that your father is proud of you, too," he said. "Goodnight, Levi. Goodnight, my Queen." He exited the vault, leaving me alone with Levi.

"Thank you," I said to my bard.

"You are welcome. I know you hate it, even if it was her," he said.

"Don't you?"

"No, because my motivation is doing it for you," he said. "And now, I'm going to take you home."

"Hmm," I said.

"What did the girls say at the salon?" he asked.

"That's a story for another time," I replied. "But I'm sure you had something to do with that little delay."

"Who me?" he asked innocently.

"Yes, you," I said, stalking toward him. "You." I poked my finger into his chest.

He grabbed my hand, leaving my finger out of his grasp. Lifting it to his mouth, I watched in anticipation. Fairy flip-flops pounded in my chest as he slid my finger in his mouth, then pulled it out slowly.

"Fuck," I muttered.

"Home," he said.

CHAPTER TWENTY-FOUR

When we arrived at the house, it was dark and quiet. I knew without asking that our children were not at home. Levi wanted the women to talk to me, so he could get the kids out of the house.

In the darkness, I could feel his breath on my neck. His heart pounded in his chest. The touch of his hand at my neck sent tingles down to my toes and back up again. He guided me backward toward the steps with his other hand on my hip. His lips hovered over mine, but he didn't give me what I wanted.

The deep blue of his eyes glittered with the spots of moonlight peeking through the curtains. Slowly, he turned me around, and we climbed the steps to our room.

"You are not leaving this house until I am done with you," he said.

"I have no intentions of leaving," I responded.

When we reached the top step, the guitar on his arm began to play the song I now recognized as our melody. Something about it reached deep inside my heart, carving a place for it to stay. I felt its magic so clearly that I knew I could play the song myself through his tattoo.

When we reached the bedroom, I pulled my sweater off over my head.

"Slow," he demanded, and I felt it inside of me. A desire to do exactly what he told me to do. My jaw dropped. A crooked smile appeared on his face.

Placing both hands on my cheeks, he looked down at me. "I swear that I will *never* make you do anything you don't want to do," he promised.

"I know that," I whispered.

"I swear it on my power." The house shook with the gravity of the vow.

"Levi."

"I will give you everything you need. I will be the man to fight by your side. The man to satisfy that fairy inside of you. The man to help raise your children."

"And what do I have to give you in return?"

"You. I just want you."

For the first time since we got home, his lips brushed over mine. I forced back my eagerness and throbbing desire. We would not rush this. At least not the first round. His hands worked the button on my jeans, as his mouth distracted me from undressing him. Slow, passionate kisses with tangled tongues and carnal moans. Each sound that I made responding to his touch caused him to chuckle or smile, even during a kiss.

Finally, I got my wits back enough to unbutton his shirt. He released me for only a moment to let it fall to the floor. I grabbed his belt, but he pushed my hands off. I'd moved too fast again. He kissed down my neck to my bra which he deftly removed.

Every kiss touched my nerve endings, firing off flares of icy numbness. As he kissed the tips of my breasts, I arched into him craving that intimate touch. It had been so long. Yet, no one had ever made me feel quite like this. The driving anticipation quelled by the one-word command. It should have been a battle inside of me, but it was more like a showy surrender instead.

He sank to his knees before me. "My Queen," he muttered as he hooked a finger into my panties, then dragged them down my legs to the floor. Starting at my knee, he kissed up my inner thigh skipping the place I wanted his lips the most.

I grunted with disapproval as he skipped it, and he grinned, keeping his eyes on me. He made his way down to my other knee and back up. Thankfully, he didn't make me wait any longer. As his lips locked on to me, my legs buckled with the intense sensation. I wasn't prepared for the intensity of the tingle to knock me off my feet, but he reacted quickly, scooping me up before I hit the floor. He laid me gently on the bed.

"Um, that must have been good," he said. He knew it was.

"It was okay," I managed to say in a breathy voice.

"I could just skip it," he suggested. I lifted my hips to his body in protest of that suggestion. "I didn't think so."

As I LAY in bed sometime in the next afternoon, I listened to Levi's breathing next to me. He didn't lie. I was completely satisfied. Levi was my King. He'd buried his song in my heart, and I don't think it could beat without it. Not ever again.

He buried quite a bit of gravy, too. I laughed at the thought of it. I'd locked legs and swapped gravy with the bard.

"Why are you awake?" he groaned.

"Thinking about gravy," I said.

"I'm out of gravy," he replied.

"I bet you aren't." I reached for him under the covers. A grin spread across his face as I found evidence of his lie.

"Do you ever stop?" he asked.

"Do you want me to stop?"

"Grace."

"Hmm?"

"I love you."

Three words that I'd heard before in my life. Words that were spoken truly and accepted. Returned truly as well, but when Levi spoke them, a chord of that song inside of me rattled with assurance.

"I love you, too." He put his hand over his heart, and he smiled.

"You feel it too?" I asked.

"Yes," he said. "I couldn't let your heart sing without mine."

My stomach took the silence as a cue to growl. He laughed.

"Did you put that there, too?" I asked.

"No, but I might have caused it," he shrugged.

"I'm going to fix breakfast," I said.

"It's past noon," he protested.

"Are you refusing bacon?" I asked.

"No, but I want you to come back to bed," he said, tugging on my arm to prevent me from getting up.

"Suck it up, Buttercup. You can't live on gravy alone!"

JOIN MY READER GROUP, Kimbra Swain's Magic and Mason Jars to get free short stories from the Trailer Park.

Want to know what happened in the salon? Join the group and read the bonus content release which will be published on February 15th, 2019.

Come on by and sit a spell! We'd love to have you.

CAST OF CHARACTERS

Grace Ann Bryant- Exiled fairy queen hiding in Shady Grove, Alabama. Daughter of Oberon. Also known as Gloriana, to her Father and the fairies of the Otherworld. She was called Hannah while traveling with the gypsy fairies before coming to North America. Owns a dachshund named Rufus. Loves orange soda and Crown. Nickname: Glory

Dylan Riggs- Sheriff of Loudon County, Alabama. Fiancé to Grace Ann Bryant. The last living Thunderbird and the only living Phoenix. Also known as Serafino Taranis and Keme Rowtag. Died saving his daughter, Winnie. Nickname: Darlin'

Levi Rearden- Changeling from Texas brought to live with Grace by Jeremiah Freyman. Given Bard powers by Oberon. Looks good in a towel. Nickname: Dublin

Wynonna Riggs- formerly known as Wynonna Jones, but adopted by Grace and Dylan. Human daughter of Bethany Jones who dies in Tinsel in a Tangle. Given the power of the Phoenix by her father. Nickname: Winnie

Aydan Thaddeus Riggs- son of Dylan Riggs and Grace Ann Bryant. Heir to Thunderbird inheritance. Rapid aging caused Aydan to seem like he's 18 years old.

Callum Fannon- Cherokee white wolf shifter. Lives with Grace and family. Calls Grace, Mom. Approx. 20 years old.

Nestor Gwinn- Grace's maternal grandfather. Kelpie. Owner of Hot Tin Roof Bar in Shady Grove. Maker of magical coffee.

Troy Maynard- Police chief in Shady Grove. Wolf shifter. Married to Amanda Capps and father to his adopted son, Mark Capps (Maynard) who is Winnie's best friend. New father to three girls.

Betty Stallworth- wife to Luther Harris. Waitress at the diner. Flirts with everyone. Fairy.

Luther Harris- head cook at the diner. Makes good gravy biscuits. Ifrit.

Tabitha Mistborne- fairy physician. Daughter of Rhiannon. Dating Remington Blake.

Mable Sanders- former spy for Oberon. Fairy Witch. Girlfriend of Nestor Gwinn.

Sergio Krykos- Grace's Uncle who has taken over the Otherworld. In his first life, he was known as Mordred, half-brother to King Arthur. Goes by the name Brockton.

Oberon- King of the Winter Otherworld. Grace's father. In his first life, he was known as King Arthur.

Rhiannon- Queen of the Summer Otherworld. Half-sister to Oberon. In her first life she was known as Morgana, a fairy witch.

Cohen- mentioned as a former king after Arthur. Grace's first human world lover. Exiled and forsaken.

Remington Blake- Grace's ex-boyfriend. Dating Tabitha Mistborne. From N'awlins. Sweet talker. One of the Native American Star-folk.

Astor Knight- The ginger knight that Grace brought back from the Summer realm. Formerly betrothed to Grace. Former First Knight of the Tree of Life. In his first life, he was Percival, Knight of the Round Table.

Soraya Harris- Jinn granddaughter of Luther Harris. Living in Shady Grove. Has connections to the world in-between life and the afterlife.

Matthew Rayburn- Druid. Spiritual leader of Shady Grove. Leads services in a Baptist Church which is a portal into the Summer Realm. Enthralled by Robin Rayburn.

Kadence Rayburn- Daughter of Matthew. Ex-girlfriend of Levi. Enthralled by Malcom Taggert. Becomes a fairy. Dating Caleb Joiner.

Malcolm Taggart- Incubus that once tried to seduce Grace. Enthralls Kady.

Caleb Joiner- Lives with Malcom and Kady, but frees Kady from Malcolm.

Riley McKenzie- Daughter of Rhiannon and Jeremiah Freyman. Levi's ex-girlfriend. Stole the songbook. Fled the Summer Realm with Grace.

Stephanie Davis- Daughter of Rhiannon. Dylan's ex-girlfriend.

Sergio Krykos' ex-girlfriend. Mother to Devin Blankenship. Missing in the Winter Otherworld.

Joey Blankenship- Tryst with Grace. Enthralled by Stephanie. Father to Devin Blankenship. Turned into a faun by Rhiannon. Escapes the Summer Realm with Grace and his son.

Eugene Jenkins- Mayor of Shady Grove. Former Knight of the Round Table, Ewain. Wife died in childbirth. Father to Ella Jenkins. Partner to Charles "Chaz" Leopold.

Eleanor "Ella" Jenkins- Changeling daughter of Mayor Jenkins. Catches Astor's eye. Teacher at the fairy school.

Charles "Chaz" Leopold- Also known as "The Lion." Hairdresser. Second Queen in Shady Grove.

Finley Bryant- Grace's "twin" brother. Married to Nelly. Wears armor portraying the symbol of Grace's royalty.

Jenny Greenteeth- A grindylow living in Shady Grove. In her first life, she was known as Guinevere, wife of Arthur, lover of Lancelot. Cursed to her current form.

Tennyson Schuyler- Mob boss. In his first life, he was known as Lancelot, Knight of the Round Table. Oberon calls him Lachlan.

Cletus and Tater Sawyer- Last human residents of Shady Grove. Comical, but full of heart.

Yule Lads- A group of Christmas Trolls who moved into town. Lamar is the most frequently mentioned with his various peg legs. Others include: Phil, Cory, Willie, Chad, Keith, Kevin, Phillip, Ryan, Bo, Richard, and Taylor.

Michean Artair- Solomonar. Owner of Magic Vape. Produces magical liquids for all occasions.

Brittany Arizona- Shady Grove's tattoo artist.

Bramble and Briar- Brownies who live in Grace's house, but are attached to Winnie. Hired by Caiaphas to watch over Grace. Now in servitude to Grace.

Caiaphas- Leader of the now defunct Sanhedrin. Former Knight of the Round Table.

Fordele and Wendy- King and Queen of the Wandering Gypsy Fairies. Fordele was Grace's lover ages ago.

Josey- Grace's former neighbor in the trailer park. Perpetually pregnant. Goddess of the Tree of Life. Also known as Lillith.

Jeremiah Freyman- Deceased. Former member of the Sanhedrin that brought Grace, Dylan, Levi, and most of the other fairies to Shady Grove. Worked for Oberon. Father of Riley. Former Knight of the Round Table. Known as Tristan.

Deacon Giles- Farmer in Shady Grove. Krampus.

Connelly Reyes- First Knight of the Fountain of Youth. Former Knight of the Round Table known as the Grail Knight, Galahad. Best friends with Astor.

Chris Purcell- Winged-werehog. Known as a dealer of information. Settled in Shady Grove with his domesticated wife, **Henrietta**.

Lissette Delphin- Creole Priestess. Tricked Levi into summoning the demon, Shanaroth.

Rowan Flanagan- Partner of Tennyson Schuyler. Died in Summer Realm. Mother of Robin Rayburn. In her first life, she was known as Elaine. Mother of Galahad.

Kyffin Merrik- Former partner in Sergio Krykos law firm. Missing.

Demetris Lysander- Grace's former lawyer. Deceased. Aswang.

Phillip Chastain- Judge at Grace's hearing in BYH. Helps with legal matters. Liaison to Human Politicians.

Misaki- Oni disguised as a Kitsune.

Elizabeth Shanteel and Colby Martin- human children murdered in BYH by Demetris Lysander.

Rev. Ezekiel Stanton- Pastor of Shady Grove Church of God. Evacuated when the humans left Shady Grove.

Sylvestor Handley- Michael Handley's father. Blacksmith.

Diego Santiago- Bear shapeshifter. Executed by Grace.

Juanita Santiago- Bear shapeshifter. Widow. Mother of two. Oversees a farm with Deacon Giles help.

Niles Babineau- Developer from New Orleans that helped Remington Blake build more housing in Shady Grove. Returned to New Orleans.

Jessica- Summer fairy working at the sheriff's office.

Stone and Bronx- Tennyson Schuyler's bodyguards.

Eogan- Treekin in Summer Realm.

Marshall- Captain of the Centaurs in Summer Realm.

Nimue- Lady of the Lake. Keeper of Excalibur. Controls the Water Element Stone.

Brad and Tonya- Brad owns the BBQ joint in Shady Grove. Tonya works there as a waitress.

Katherine Frist- Fairy woman living in Shady Grove known for her many dead husbands.

Ellessa- Grace's Siren mother. Whereabouts unknown.

Melissa Marx- Levi fangirl.

Taleisin- Bard for Arthur and many other Kings and Rulers. Wrote the songbook given to Levi.

Thistle- Purple haired pixie with a love envelope.

Sandy- Matthew Rayburn's Nurse

Zahir- former knight of the round table, Palamedes. Exiled and forsaken for choosing Lancelot's side. Jinn.

Madam Luella Specter- Griffin breeder, also known as Lulu

Tashi- yeti brewmaster

ACKNOWLEDGMENTS

To my wonderful husband, Jeff, who one day said, you need to have a character that is a Sasquatch. And, he needs to brew his own beer in his backpack. So, Tashi is the creation of my husband. My very own Sasquatch.

Thanks to all my BETA, ARC, and reader groups. You guys are the reason I keep pushing. You love Grace. I love Grace. It's a perfect relationship.

Thanks to my professional crew. Carol, my editor. Thanks to Audrey who took on the huge project of rebranding FToaTPQ. And even though I'm doing my own formats now, Ericka is still there answering my questions.

Finally thanks to all the squirrels on the University of Alabama campus. I've always believed you were supernatural creatures.

ABOUT THE AUTHOR

From early in life Kimbra Swain was indoctrinated in the ways of geekdom. Raised on Star Wars, Tolkien, Superheroes, and Voltron, she found herself immersed in a world of imagination. She started writing in high school, and completed her English degree from the University of Alabama in 2003.

Her writing is influenced by a gamut of authors including Jane Austen, J.R.R. Tolkien, L.M. Montgomery, Timothy Zahn, Kathy Reichs, Kevin Hearne, and Jim Butcher.

Born and raised in Alabama, Kimbra still lives there with her husband and 6-year-old daughter.

Follow Kimbra on Facebook, Twitter, and
Instagram.
www.kimbraswain.com
www.fairytalesofatrailerparkqueen.com

Abomination: The Path to Redemption Series, Book 1

Frivolous Magic: Chantilly Lace, Book 1

The next book in the series is Suck It Up, Buttercup! Download it today!

Join my reader group for updates on all my books and exclusive bonus content: Kimbra Swain's Magic and Mason Jars

Made in the USA
Monee, IL
22 September 2020